Adam Lindsay Gordon

Ashtaroth; a Dramatic Lyric

Adam Lindsay Gordon

Ashtaroth; a Dramatic Lyric

ISBN/EAN: 9783744769259

Printed in Europe, USA, Canada, Australia, Japan

Cover: Foto ©Andreas Hilbeck / pixelio.de

More available books at **www.hansebooks.com**

ASHTAROTH; A DRAMATIC LYRIC.

ASHTAROTH;

A DRAMATIC LYRIC.

BY

THE AUTHOR OF "SEA SPRAY AND SMOKE DRIFT."

MELBOURNE:

CLARSON, MASSINA, & CO., PRINTERS AND PUBLISHERS.

SYDNEY: GIBBS, SHALLARD, & CO.

1867.

DRAMATIS PERSONÆ.

HUGO, *a Norman Baron and a scholar.*

ERIC, *a friend of Hugo's.*

THURSTON,
EUSTACE, } *Followers of Hugo.*
RALPH,

HENRY, *a Page.*

LUKE,
HUBERT, } *Monks living in a Norman Chapel.*

BASIL, *Abbot of a Convent on the Rhine.*

CYRIL, *a Monk of the same Convent.*

OSRIC, *a Norwegian Adventurer, and formerly a Corsair.*

RUDOLPH, *an Outlawed Count, and the Captain of a Band of Robbers.*

DAGOBERT, *the Captain of some predatory Soldiers called "Free Lances."*

HAROLD, *a Danish Knight.*

ORION.

THORA,
AGATHA,
ELSPETH, *a Nurse of Thora's,* } WOMEN.
URSULA, *Abbess of the Convent on the Rhine,*
NUNS, ETC.,

Men-at-Arms, Soldiers, and Robbers; Monks, Friars, and Churchmen; Spirits, etc.

ASHTAROTH.

SCENE—A CASTLE IN NORMANDY. *A Study in a Tower;* HUGO
  *seated at a table covered with maps and charts of the heavens,
  astronomical instruments, books, manuscripts, etc.*

Enter HENRY, *a Page.*

HUGO :

Well, boy, what is it ?

HENRY :   The feast is spread.

HUGO :

Why tarry the guests for me ?
Let Eric sit at the table's head ;
  Alone I desire to be. ·   [HENRY *goes out.*
What share have I at their festive board,
  Their mirth I can only mar ;
To me no pleasure their cups afford,
  Their songs on my silence jar.
With an aching eye and a throbbing brain,
  And yet with a hopeful heart,
I must toil and strain with the planets again
  When the rays of the sun depart ;
He who must needs with the topers tope,
  And the feasters feast in the hall,
How can he hope with a matter to cope
  That is immaterial !

ORION :

He who his appetite stints and curbs
  Shut up in the northern wing,

B

With his rye-bread flavoured with bitter herbs,
    And his draught from the tasteless spring,
Good sooth, he is but a sorry clown.
    There are some good things upon earth—
Pleasure and power and fair renown,
    And wisdom of worldly worth;
There is wisdom in follies that charm the sense,
    In follies that light the eyes,
But the folly to wisdom that makes pretence
    Is alone by the fool termed wise.

HUGO:

    Thy speech, Orion, is somewhat rude;
        Perchance having jeer'd and scoff'd
    To thy fill, thou wilt curb thy jeering mood;
        I wot thou hast served me oft.
    This plan of the skies seems fairly traced;
        What errors canst thou detect?

ORION:

    Nay, the constellations are all misplaced
        And the satellites incorrect;
    Leave the plan to me; you have time to seek
        An hour of needful rest,
    The night is young, and the planets are weak:
        See, the sun still reddens the west.

HUGO:

    I fear I shall sleep too long.

ORION: If you do
        It matters not much; the sky
    Is cloudy, the stars will be faint and few;
        Now, list to my lullaby.

        (Sings.)   [HUGO reclines on a couch.

            Still the darkling skies are red,
                Though the day-god's course is run;
            Heavenly night lamps overhead
                Flash and twinkle one by one.

Idle dreamer, earth-born elf!
　Vainly grasping heavenly things,
Wherefore weariest thou thyself
　With thy vain imaginings?

From the tree of knowledge first,
　Since his parents pluck'd the fruit,
Man, with partial knowledge curs'd,
　Of the tree still seeks the root;
Musty volumes crowd thy shelf—
　Which of these true knowledge brings?
Wherefore weariest thou thyself
　With thy vain imaginings?

Will the stars from heaven descend?
　Can the earth-worm soar and rise?
Can the mortal comprehend
　Heaven's own hallow'd mysteries?
Greed and glory, power and pelf—
　These are won by clowns and kings;
Wherefore weariest thou thyself
　With thy vain imaginings?

Sow and reap, and toil and spin;
　Eat and drink, and dream and die;
Man may strive, yet never win,
　And I laugh the while and cry—
Idle dreamer—earth-born elf!
　Vainly grasping heavenly things,
Wherefore weariest thou thyself
　With thy vain imaginings?

He sleeps, and his sleep appears serene,
　Whatever dreams it has brought him—

　　　　　　　　　[Looks at the plans.

If he knows what those hieroglyphics mean,
　He's wiser than one who taught him.
Why does he number the Pole-star thus,
　Or the Pleiades why combine?
And what is he doing with Sirius!
　In the devil's name or in mine?
Man thinks discarding the beaten track,
　That the sins of his youth are slain,
When he seeks fresh sins, but he soon comes back
　To his old pet sins again.

SCENE—The Same.   Hugo *waking*, Orion *seated near him.*
Daybreak.

HUGO :

    Oh ! weary spirit, Oh ! cloudy eyes,
       Oh ! heavy and misty brain !
    Yon riddle that lies 'twixt earth and skies,
       Ye seek to explore in vain !
    See the east is grey ; put those scrolls away,
       And hide them far from my sight ;
    I will toil and study no more by day,
       I will watch no longer by night ;
    I have labour'd and long'd, and now I seem
       No nearer the mystic goal ;
    Orion, I fain would devise some scheme
       To quiet this restless soul ;
    To distant climes I would fain depart—
       I would travel by sea or land.

ORION :

    Nay, I warn'd you of this, " Short life, long art,"
       The proverb, though stale, will stand ;
    Full many a sage from youth to age
       Has toil'd to attain what you
    Would master at once.   In a pilgrimage,
       Forsooth, there is nothing new,
    Though virtue, I ween, in change of scene,
       And vigour in change of air,
    Will always be, and has always been,
       And travel is a tonic rare ;
    Still, the restless discontented mood
       For the time alone is eased,
    It will soon return with hunger renew'd
       And appetite unappeased.
    Nathless I could teach a shorter plan
       To win that wisdom you crave ;
    That lore that is seldom attain'd by man
       From the cradle down to the grave.

HUGO :

    Such lore I had rather do without, .
    It has nothing mystic nor awful
    In my eyes.   Nay, I despise and doubt
      The arts that are term'd unlawful ;
    'Twixt science and magic the line lies plain.
      I shall never wittingly pass it ;
    There is now no compact between us twain.

ORION :   But an understanding tacit ;

    You have prosper'd much since the day we met ;
      You were then a landless knight,
    You now have honour and wealth, and yet
      I never can serve you right.

HUGO :

    Enough ; we will start this very day,
      Thurston, Eric, and I,
    And the baffled visions will pass away,
      And the restless fires will die.

ORION :

    Till the fuel expires that feeds those fires
      They smoulder and live unspent ;
    Give a mortal all that his heart desires
      He is less than ever content.

SCENE—A CLIFF ON THE BRETON COAST, OVERHANGING THE SEA.
HUGO.

HUGO :

    Down drops the red sun ; through the gloaming
      They burst—raging waves of the sea
    Foaming out their own shame—ever foaming
      Their leprosy up with fierce glee ;
    Flung back from the stone, snowy fountains
      Of feathery flakes, scarcely flag
    Where shock after shock, the green mountains
      Explode on the iron-grey crag.

The salt spray with ceaseless commotion
　　Leaps round me.　I sit on the verge
Of the cliff—'twixt the earth and the ocean—
　　With feet overhanging the surge;
In thy grandeur, oh sea! we acknowledge,
　　In thy fairness, oh earth! we confess,
Hidden truths that are taught in no college,
　　Hidden songs that no parchments express.

Were they wise in their own generations,
　　Those sages and sagas of old?
They have pass'd; o'er their names and their
　　　nations
Time's billows have silently roll'd;
They have pass'd, leaving little to their children
　　Save histories of a truth far from strict;
Or theories more vague and bewild'ring
　　Since three out of four contradict.

Lost labour! vain book-worms have sat in
　　The halls of dull pedants who teach
Strange tongues, the dead lore of the Latin,
　　The scroll that is god-like and Greek;
Have wasted life's springtide in learning
　　Things long ago learnt all in vain;
They are slow, very slow, in discerning
　　That book lore and wisdom are twain.

Pale shades of a creed that was mythic,
　　By time or by truth overcome,
Your Delphian temples and Pythic
　　Are ruins deserted and dumb;
Your Muses are hush'd, and your Graces
　　Are bruised and defaced; and your gods
Enshrin'd and enthroned in high places
　　No longer, are powerless as clods;

By forest and streamlet, where glisten'd
　Fair feet of the Naiads that skimm'd
The shallows; where the Oreads listened
　Rose-lipp'd, amber-hair'd, marble-limb'd,
No lithe forms disport in the river,
　No sweet faces peer through the boughs;
Elms and beeches wave silent for ever,
　Ever silent the bright water flows.   ·

(Were they duller or wiser than we are,
　Those heathens of old?   Who shall say?
Worse or better?   Thy wisdom, oh " Thea
　Glaucopis" was wise in thy day,
And the false gods alluring to evil,
　That sway'd reckless votaries then,
Were slain to no purpose: they revel
　Recrowned in the hearts of us men.)

Dead priests of Osiris, and Isis,
　And Apis! that mystical lore,
Like a nightmare, conceived in a crisis
　Of fever, is studied no more;
Dead Magian! yon star-troop that spangles
　The arch of yon firmament vast
Looks calm, like a host of white angels,
　On dry dust of votaries past.

On seas unexplored can the ship shun
　Sunk rocks?   Can man fathom life's links,
Past or future, unsolved by Egyptian
　Or Theban, unspoken by Sphynx,
The riddle remains, still unravell'd,
　By student consuming night oil.
Oh earth! we have toil'd, we have travail'd:
　How long shall we travail and toil?

How long ?   The short life that fools reckon
    So sweet, by how much is it higher
Than brute life ? the false gods still beckon,
    And man, through the dust and the mire,
Toils onward, as toils the dull bullock,
    Unreasoning, brutish, and blind,
With Ashtaroth, Mammon, and Moloch
    In front, and Alecto behind.

The wise one of earth, the Chaldæan
    Serves folly in wisdom's disguise ;
And the sensual Epicuræan
    Though grosser, is hardly less wise,
'Twixt the former, half-pedant, half-pagan,
    And the latter, half sow and half sloth,
We halt, choose Astarté or Dagon,
    Or sacrifice freely to both.

With our reason that seeks to disparage
    Brute instinct it fails to subdue ;
With our false illegitimate courage,
    Our sophistry, vain and untrue ;
Our hopes, that ascend so and fall so,
    Our passions, fierce hates and hot loves,
We are wise (ay, the snake is wise also)—
    Wise as serpents, *not* harmless as doves.

Some flashes, like faint sparks from heaven,
    Come rarely with rushing of wings ;
We are conscious at times, we have striven,
    Though seldom, to grasp better things ;
These pass, leaving hearts that have falter'd,
    Good angels with faces estranged,
And the skin of the Ethiop unalter'd
    And the spots of the leopard unchanged.

Oh earth ! pleasant earth ! have we hanker'd
　　To gather thy flowers and thy fruits ?
The roses are wither'd, and canker'd
　　The lilies, and barren the roots
Of the fig-tree, the vine, the wild olive,
　　Sharp thorns and sad thistles that yield
Fierce harvest—so *we* live and *so* live
　　The perishing beasts of the field—

And withal we are conscious of evil
　　And good—of the spirit and the clod,
Of the power in our hearts of a devil,
　　Of the power in our souls of a God
Whose commandments are graven in no cypher,
　　But clear as his sun—from our youth
One at least we have cherish'd—" An eye for
　　An eye and a tooth for a tooth."

Oh man ! of thy Maker the image ;
　　To passion, to pride, or to wealth,
Sworn bondsman, from dull youth to dim age,
　　Thy portion, the fire or the filth,
Dross seeking ; dead pleasure's death rattle
　　Thy memories' happiest song
And thy highest hope—scarce a drawn battle
　　With dark desperation.　How long ?

　　．　　　．　　　．　　　．　　　．　　　．

Roar louder ! leap higher ! ye surf-beds,
　　And sprinkle your foam on the furze ;
Bring the dreams that brought sleep to our turf-beds,
　　To camps of our long ago years,
With the flashing and sparkling of broadswords,
　　With the tossing of banners and spears,
With the trampling of hard hoofs on hard swards,
　　With the mingling of trumpets and cheers.

The gale has gone down ; yet outlasting
    The gale, raging waves of the sea
Casting up their own foam, ever casting
    Their leprosy up with wild glee,
Still storm ; so in rashness and rudeness,
    Man storms through the days of his grace ;
Yet man cannot fathom God's goodness,
    Exceeding God's infinite space ;

And coldly and calmly and purely
    Grey rock and green hillock lie white
In a star-shine dream-laden—so surely
    Night cometh—so cometh the night
When we, too, at peace with our neighbour,
    May sleep where God's hillocks are piled,
Thanking HIM for a rest from day's labour,
    And a sleep like the sleep of a child !

SCENE—THE CASTLE IN NORMANDY.   THORA *working at embroidery,*
            ELSPETH *spinning.*

THORA (*sings*) :

We severed in Autumn early,
    Ere the earth was torn by the plough ;
The wheat and the oats and the barley
    Are ripe for the harvest now.
We sunder'd one misty morning
    Ere the hills were dimm'd by the rain ;
Through the flowers those hills adorning
    Thou comest not back again.

My heart is heavy and weary
    With the weight of a weary soul ;
The mid-day glare groweth dreary,
    And dreary the midnight scroll,
The corn-stalks sigh for the sickle
    'Neath the load of their golden grain ;
I sigh for a mate more fickle—
    Thou comest not back again.

The warm sun riseth and setteth,
    The night bringeth moist'ning dew,
But the soul that longeth, forgetteth
    The warmth and the moisture, too ;
In the hot sun rising and setting
    There is naught save feverish pain ;
There are tears in the night-dews wetting—
    Thou comest not back again.

Thy voice in mine ear still mingles
    With the voices of whisp'ring trees,
Thy kiss on my cheek still tingles
    At each kiss of the summer breeze ;
While dreams of the past are thronging
    For substance of shades·in vain,
I am waiting, watching, and longing—
    Thou comest not back again.

Waiting and watching ever,
    Longing and lingering yet,
Leaves rustle and corn-stalks quiver,
    Winds murmur and waters fret ;
No answer they bring, no greeting,
    No speech, save that sad refrain,
No voice, save an echo repeating—
    He cometh not back again.

ELSPETH :

Thine eldest sister is wedded to Max ;
    With Biorn, Hilda hath cast her lot.
If the husbands vanish'd, and left no tracks,
    Would the wives have cause for sorrow, I wot ?

THORA :

How well I remember that dreary ride ;
    How I sigh'd for the lands of ice and snow,
In the trackless wastes of the desert wide,
    With the sun o'erhead and the sand below ;
'Neath the scanty shade of the feathery palms,
    How I sigh'd for the forest of sheltering firs,
Whose shadows environ'd the Danish farms
    Where I sang and sported in childish years.
On the fourteenth day of our pilgrimage
    We stay'd at the foot of a sandhill high ;

Our fever'd thirst we could scarce assuage
    At the brackish well that was nearly dry;
And the hot sun rose, and the hot sun set,
    And we rode all the day through a desert land,
And we camp'd where the lake and the river met,
    On sedge and shingle and shining sand;
Enfolded in Hugo's cloak I slept,
    Or watch'd the stars while I lay awake;
And close to our feet the staghound crept
    And the horses were grazing beside the lake;
Now we own castles and serving men,
    Lands and revenues.   What of that?
Hugo the Norman was kinder then,
    And happier was Thora of Armorat.

ELSPETH:

Nay, I warn'd thee, with Norman sails unfurl'd
    Above our heads, when we wished thee joy,
That men are the same all over the world;
    They will worship only the newest toy;
Yet Hugo is kind and constant, too,
    Though somewhat given to studies of late;
Biorn is sottish, and Max untrue,
    And worse than thine is thy sister's fate.
But a shadow darkens the chamber door.

Enter THURSTON.

THURSTON:

'Tis I, Lady Thora; our lord is near.
My horse being fresher, I rode before;
    Both he and Eric will soon be here.

THORA:

Good Thurston, give me your hand. You are
    Most welcome. What has delay'd you thus?

THURSTON:

Both by sea and land we have travell'd far,
    Yet little of note has happen'd to us—

We were wreck'd on the shores of Brittany,
   Near the coast of Morbihan iron-bound ;
The rocks were steep and the surf ran high,
   Thy kinsman, Eric, was well nigh drown'd.
By a swarm of knaves we were next beset,
   Who took us for corsairs ; then released
By a Breton count, whose name I forget.
   Now, I go, by your leave, to tend my beast.
                    [*He goes out.*

ELSPETH :
   That man is rude and froward of speech :
   My ears are good, though my sight grows dim.
THORA :
   Thurston is faithful.   Thou canst not teach
   Courtly nor servile manners to him.

SCENE—THE CASTLE HALL.   THURSTON, RALPH, EUSTACE, *and other
followers of* HUGO, *seated at a long table.* HAROLD *seated apart.*

THURSTON :
   Who is that stranger, dark and tall,
   On the wooden settle next to the wall :
   Mountebank, pilgrim, or wandering bard ?
EUSTACE :
   To define his calling is somewhat hard ;
   Lady Thora has taken him by the hand
   Because he has come from the Holy Land.
   Pilgrims and palmers are all the rage
   With her, since she shared in that pilgrimage
   With Hugo.   The stranger came yesterday,
   And would have gone on, but she bade him stay.
   Besides, he sings in the Danish tongue
   The songs she has heard in her childhood sung.

That's all I know of him, good or bad,
In my own opinion, he's somewhat mad.
You must raise your voice if you speak with him,
And he answers as though his senses were dim.

THURSTON (*to Harold*) :

Good morrow, sir stranger.

HAROLD :

      Good morrow, friend.

THURSTON :

Where do you come from ? and whither wend ?

HAROLD :

I have travelled, of late, with the setting sun
At my back ; and as soon as my task is done
I purpose to turn my face to the North.
Yet we know not what a day may bring forth.

THURSTON :

Indeed we don't.
 (*To* EUSTACE, *aside*) Nay, I know him now
By that ugly scar that crosses his brow,
And the less we say to him the better.
Your judgment is right to the very letter—
The man is mad—

EUSTACE :   But harmless, I think ;
He eats but little, eschews strong drink,
And only speaks when spoken to first.

THURSTON :

Harmless or not, he was once the worst
And bitterest foe Lord Hugo had ;
And yet his story is somewhat sad—

EUSTACE :

May I hear it ?

THURSTON :   Nay, I never reveal
What concerns me not. Our lord may conceal
Or divulge at pleasure his own affairs,—
Not even his comrade Eric shares

His secrets ; though Eric thinks him wise,
Which is more than I do, for I despise
That foolish science he learnt at Rome.
He dreams and mopes when he sits at home,
And now he's not much better abroad ;
'Tis hard to follow so tame a lord.
'Twixt us two, he won't be worth a rush
If he will persist in his studies—

EUSTACE :   Hush !
Ralph has persuaded our guest to sing.

THURSTON :
I have known the day when his voice would ring
Till the rafters echoed.

EUSTACE :   'Tis pleasant still,
Though far too feeble this hall to fill.

HAROLD (*sings*) :

On the current, where the wide
    Windings of the river
Eddy to the North Sea tide,
Shall I in my shallop glide,
As I have done at her side ?—
    Never ! never ! never !

In the forest, where the firs,
    Pines and larches quiver
To the northern breeze that stirs,
Shall my lips be press'd to hers,
As they were in bygone years ?—
  . Never ! never ! never !

In the battle on the plain,
    Where the lance-shafts shiver,
And the sword-strokes fall like rain,
Shall I bear her scarf again
As I have done ?—not in vain—
    Never ! never ! never ?

In a fairer, brighter land,
    Where the saints rest ever,
Shall I once more see her stand,
White, amidst a white-robed band,
Harp and palm-branch in her hand ?
    Never ! never ! never !

SCENE—The Same. Eustace, Thurston, *and followers of* Hugo.
HAROLD.

Enter by the hall door, Hugo, Eric, *and* Thora.

EUSTACE (*and others standing up*):
    Welcome, Lord Hugo !
HUGO :   Welcome or not,
    Thanks for your greeting all.
    Ha, Eustace ! what complaints hast thou got ?
    What grievances to recall ?
EUSTACE :
    Count William came with a numerous band,
      Ere the snows began to fall,
    And slew a buck on your lordship's land,
      Within a league of the wall.
HUGO :
    Count William has done to us no more
      Than we to him. In his vineyard
    Last summer, or later may be, a boar
      Was slaughter'd by Thurston's whinyard.
THURSTON :
    Ay, Hugo ! But William kept the buck
      I will wager marks a score,
    Though the tale is new to me ; and, worse luck,
      You made me give back the boar.
HAROLD (*advancing*):
    Lord Hugo !
HUGO :   What ! Art thou living yet !
    I scarcely knew thee, Sir Dane !
    And 'tis not so very long since we met.
HAROLD :
      'Twill be long ere we meet again; (*gives a letter*)
    This letter was traced by one now dead
      In the Holy Land; and I
    Must wait till his dying request is read.
      And in his name ask the reply.

THORA (*aside*):

    Who is that stranger, Hugo ?

HUGO :   By birth

    He is countryman of thine,

    Thora : what writing is this on earth ?

    I can scarce decipher a line.

HAROLD :

    The pen in the clutch of death works ill.

HUGO :

    Nay, I read now ; the letters run

    More clearly.

HAROLD :   Wilt grant the request ?

HUGO :   I will.

HAROLD :

    Enough ! Then my task is done. (*He holds*
        out his hand)

    Hugo, I go to a far off land,

    Wilt thou say, " God speed thee !" now ?

HUGO :

    Sir Harold, I cannot take thy hand,

    Because of my ancient vow.

HAROLD :

    Farewell, then.

THORA :   Friend, till the morning wait.

    On so wild a night as this

    Thou shalt not go from my husband's gate,

    The path thou wilt surely miss.

HAROLD :

    I go. Kind lady, some future day

    Thy care will requited be.

THORA :

    Speak, Hugo, speak !

HUGO :   He may go or stay,

    It matters little to me.

                      [HAROLD *goes out.*

C

THORA :

    Husband, that man is ill and weak ;
      On foot he goes and alone
    Through a barren moor in a night-storm bleak.

ERIC :

    Now, I wonder where he has gone !

HUGO :

    Indeed, I have not the least idea ;
      The man is certainly mad.
    He wedded my sister, Dorothea,
      And used her cruelly bad.
    He was once my firmest and surest friend,
      And once my deadliest foe ;
    But hate and friendship both find their end—
      Now I heed not where he may go.

SCENE—A CHAMBER IN THE CASTLE. HUGO, THORA, *and* ERIC.

HUGO :

    That letter that came from Palestine
      By the hands of yon wandering Dane,
    Will cost me a pilgrimage to the Rhine.

THORA :

    Wilt thou travel so soon again ?

HUGO :

    I can scarce refuse the dying request
      Of my comrade, Baldwin, now ;
    His bones are dust.   May his soul find rest !
      He once made a foolish vow
    That at Engelmehr, 'neath the watchful care
      Of the Abbess his child should stay,
    For a season at least.   To escort her there
      I must start at the break of day.

THORA :

>Is it Agatha that goes or Clare ?

HUGO :

>Nay, Clare is dwelling in Spain
>With her spouse.

THORA :   'Tis Agatha.   She is fair

>I am told ; but giddy and vain.

ERIC :

>Some musty tales on my memory grow
>>Concerning Count Baldwin's vow.
>Thou knew'st his daughter ?

HUGO :   Ay, years ago.

>I should scarcely know her now.
>It seems when her father's vow was made
>>She was taken sorely ill ;
>Then he travell'd, and on his return was stay'd ;
>>He could never his oath fulfil.

ERIC :

>If rightly I've heard 'twas Agatha
>>That fled with some Danish knight—
>I forget the name.

HUGO :

>>>Nay, she fled not far,
>She returned again that night.

THORA :

>For a nun, I fear she is too self-willed.

HUGO :

>That is no affair of mine.
>My task is over, my word fulfilled,
>>Should I bring her safe to the Rhine.
>Come, Thora, sing.

THORA :   Nay, I cannot sing,

>Nor would I now, if I could.
>Sing thou.

HUGO :   I will, though my voice should bring
       No sound save a discord rude.

(*Sings.*)

> Where the storm in its wrath hath lighted,
>   The pine lies low in the dust ;
> And the corn is withered and blighted,
>   Where the fields are red with the rust ;
> Falls the black frost, nipping and killing,
>   Where its petals the violet rears,
> And the wind, though tempered, is chilling
>   To the lamb despoiled by the shears.
>
> The strong in their strength are shaken,
>   The wise in their wisdom fall ;
> And the bloom of beauty is taken—
>   Strength, wisdom, beauty, and all ;
> They vanish, their lot fulfilling,
>   Their doom approaches and nears,
> But the wind, though tempered, is chilling
>   To the lamb despoiled by the shears.
>
> 'Tis the will of a Great Creator,
>   He is wise, His will must be done,
> And it cometh sooner or later ;
>   And one shall be taken, and one
> Shall be left here, toiling and tilling
>   In this vale of sorrows and tears,
> Where the wind, though tempered, is chilling
>   To the lamb despoiled by the shears.
>
> Tell me, mine own one, tell me.
>   The shadows of life and the fears
> Shall neither daunt me nor quell me,
>   While I can avert thy tears :
> Dost thou shrink, as I shrink, unwilling
>   To realise lonely years ?
> Since the wind, though tempered, is chilling
>   To the lamb despoiled by the shears.

Enter HENRY.

HENRY :

My lord, Father Luke craves audience straight,
   He has come on foot from the chapel ;
Some stranger perished beside his gate,
   When the dawn began to dapple.

SCENE—A Chapel not very far from Hugo's Castle. Hugo,
Eric, *and two Monks* (Luke *and* Hubert). *The dead body of*
Harold.

Luke :

When the dawn was breaking,
Came a faint sound, waking
Hubert and myself; we hurried to the door,
Found the stranger lying
At the threshold, dying.
Somewhere have I seen a face like his before.

Hugo :

Harold he is hight,
Only yesternight
From our gates he wandered, in the driving hail ;
Well his face I know,
Both as friend and foe ;
Of my followers only Thurston knows his tale.

Luke :

Few the words he said,
Faint the signs he made,
Twice or thrice he groaned, quoth Hubert, " Thou
        hast sinn'd.
This is retribution,
Seek for absolution ;
Answer me—then cast thy sorrows to the wind.
Do their voices reach thee ?
Friends who failed to teach thee,
In thine earlier days, to sunder right from wrong,
Charges 'gainst thee cited,
Cares all unrequited,
Counsels spurned and slighted—do they press
        and throng ?"
But he shook his head.
" 'Tis not so," he said ;
" They will scarce reproach me who reproached
        of yore.

If their counsel 's good,
Rashly I withstood ;
Having suffered longer, I have suffered more."

"Do their curses stun thee?
Foes who failed to shun thee,
Stricken by rash vengeance, in some wild career.
As the barbed arrow
Cleaveth bone and marrow
From those chambers narrow—do they pierce
        thine ear ?"
And he made reply,
Laughing bitterly,
"Did I fear them living—shall I fear them dead ?
Blood that I have spilt
Leaveth little guilt ;
On the hand it resteth, scarcely on the head."

"Is there one whom thou
May'st have wronged ere now,
Since remorse so sorely weigheth down thine
        heart ?
By some saint in heaven,
Sanctified and shriven,
Would'st thou be forgiven ere thy soul depart ?"
Not a word he said,
But he bowed his head
Till his temples rested on the chilly sods ;
And we heard him groan—
"Ah ! mine own, mine own !
If I had thy pardon I might ask for God's."

Hubert raised him slowly.
Sunrise, faint and holy,
Lit the dead face, placid as a child's might be.

May the troubled spirit,
Through Christ's saving merit,
Peace and rest inherit.   Thus we sent for thee.

HUGO :

God o'erruleth fate.
I had cause for hate :
In this very chapel, years back, proud and strong ;
Joined by priestly vows,
He became the spouse
Of my youngest sister, to her bitter wrong.
And he wrought her woe,
Making me his foe ;
Not alone unfaithful—brutal, too, was he.
She had scarce been dead
Three months ere he fled
With Count Baldwin's daughter, then betrothed
        to me.
Fortune straight forsook him,
Vengeance overtook him ;
Heavy crimes will bring down heavy punishment.
All his strength was shatter'd,
Even his wits were scatter'd,
Half-deranged, half-crippled, wandering he went.
We are unforgiving
While our foes are living ;
Yet his retribution weigh'd so heavily
That I feel remorse
Gazing on his corse,
For my rudeness when he left our gates to die.
And his grave shall be
'Neath the chestnut tree
Where he met my sister many years ago ;
Leave that tress of hair
On his bosom there—
Wrap the cerecloth round him !   Eric, let us go.

SCENE—A Room in the Castle. Hugo and Eric. *Early morning.*

Hugo:

    The morn is fair, the weary miles
    Will shorten 'neath the summer's wiles,
    Pomona in the orchard smiles,
    And in the meadow, Flora;
    And I have roused a chosen band
    For escort through the troubled land;
    And shaken Elspeth by the hand,
    And said farewell to Thora.
    Comrade and kinsman—for thou art
    Comrade and kin to me—we part
    Ere nightfall, if at once we start,
    We gain the dead Count's castle.
    The roads are fair, the days are fine,
    Ere long I hope to reach the Rhine.
    Forsooth, no friend to me or mine
    Is that same Abbot Basil;
    I thought he wrong'd us by his greed.
    My father sign'd a foolish deed
    For lack of gold in time of need,
    And thus our lands went by us;
    Yet wrong on our side may have been;
    As far as my will goes, I ween,
    'Tis pass'd, the grudge that lay between
    Us twain.   Men call him pious—
    And I have prosper'd much since then,
    And gain'd for one lost acre ten;
    And even the ancient house and glen
    Rebought with purchase-money.
    He, too, is wealthy; he has got
    By churchly right a fertile spot,
    A land of corn and wine, I wot,
    A land of milk and honey.

Now, Eric, change thy plans and ride
With us, thou hast no ties, no bride.

ERIC:

Nay, ties I have, and time and tide
Thou knowest wait for no man;
And I go north; God's blessing shuns
The dwellings of forgetful sons,
That proverb he may read who runs,
In Christian lore or Roman.
My good old mother, she hath heard,
For twelve long months, from me no word;
At thought of her my heart is stirr'd,
And even mine eyes grow moister.
Greet Ursula from me; her fame
Is known to all. A nobler dame,
Since days of Clovis, ne'er became
The inmate of a cloister.
Our paths diverge, yet we may go
Together for a league or so;
I, too, will join thy band below
When thou thy bugle windest.

[ERIC *goes out.*

HUGO:

From weaknesses we stand afar,
On us unpleasantly they jar;
And yet the stoutest-hearted one,
The gentlest and the kindest.
My mother loved me tenderly;
Alas! her only son was I.
I shudder'd, but my lids were dry,
By death made orphan newly.
A braver man than me, I swear,
Who never comprehended fear,
Scarce names his mother, and the tear,
Unbidden, springs, unruly.

SCENE—A Road on the Norman Frontiers. Hugo, Agatha, Orion, Thurston, *and armed attendants, riding slowly.*

AGATHA :

Sir Knight, what makes you so grave and glum,
At times, I fear you are deaf or dumb,
Or both.

HUGO :   And yet, should I speak the truth,
There is little in common 'twixt us, forsooth,
You would think me duller, and still more vain,
If I uttered the thoughts that fill my brain ;
Since the matters with which my mind is laden
Would scarcely serve to amuse a maiden.

AGATHA :

I am so foolish, and you are so wise,
'Tis the meaning your words so ill disguise.
Alas ! my prospects are sad enough :
I had rather listen to speeches rough,
Than muse and meditate silently
On the coming loss of my liberty.
Sad hope to me can my future bring,
Yet, while I may, I would prattle and sing,
Though it only were to try and assuage
The dreariness of my pilgrimage.

HUGO :

Prattle and sing to your heart's content,
And none will offer impediment.

AGATHA (*sings*) :

We were playmates in childhood, my sister and I,
  Whose playtime with childhood is done ;
Through thickets where briar and bramble grew high,
  Barefooted I've oft seen her run.

I've known her when mists on the moorland hung white,
  Bareheaded past nightfall remain ;
She has followed a landless and penniless knight
  Through battles and sieges in Spain.

But I pulled the flower, and shrank from the thorn,
  Sought the sunshine, and fled from the mist;
My sister was born to face hardship with scorn—
  I was born to be fondled and kiss'd.

HUGO (*aside*):

  She has a sweet voice.

ORION :   And a sweet face, too—

  Be candid for once, and give her her due.

AGATHA :

  Your face grows longer, and still more long,
  Sir Scholar ! how did you like my song ?

HUGO :

  I thought it rather a silly one.

AGATHA :

  You are far from a pleasant companion.

SCENE—An Apartment in a Wayside Inn. Hugo and Agatha.
Evening.

HUGO :

  I will leave you now—we have talked enough,
    And for one so tenderly reared and nursed
  This journey is wearisome, perhaps, and rough.

AGATHA :   Will you not finish your story first ?

HUGO :

  I repent me that I began it now,
    'Tis a dismal tale for a maiden's ears ;
  Your cheek is pale already, your brow
    Is sad, and your eyes are moist with tears.

AGATHA :

  It may be thus, I am lightly vexed,
    But the tears will lightly come and go ;
  I can cry one moment and laugh the next,
    Yet I have seen terrors, as well you know.
  I remember that flight through moss and fern,
    The moonlit shadows, the hoofs that rolled

In fierce pursuit, and the ending stern,
  And the hawk that left his prey on the wold.
HUGO :
I have sorrowed since that I left you there :
  Your friends were close behind on the heath,
Though not so close as I thought they were.
  (*Aside*)   Now I will not tell her of Harold's death.
AGATHA :
'Tis true I was justly punished, and men,
  As a rule, of pity have little share :
Had I died, you had cared but little then.
HUGO :   But little then, yet now I should care
More than you think for.   Now, good night.
    Tears still ?   Ere I leave you, child, alone,
Must I dry your cheeks ?
AGATHA :   Nay, I am not quite
  Such a child, but what I can dry my own.

                    [HUGO *goes out.*   AGATHA *retires.*

ORION (*singing outside the window of* AGATHA'S *chamber*):

'Neath the stems with blossoms laden,
  'Neath the tendrils curling,
I, thy servant, sing, oh, maiden !
  I, thy slave, oh, darling !
Lo ! the shaft that slew the red deer,
  At the elk may fly too,
Spare them not !   The dead are dead, dear,
  Let the living die too.

Where the wiles of serpent mingle,
  And the looks of dove lie,
Where small hands in strong hands tingle,
  Loving eyes meet lovely ;
Where the harder natures soften,
  And the softer, harden—
Certes ! such things have been often,
  Since we left Eve's garden.

Sweeter follies herald sadder
  Sins—look not too closely ;
Tongue of asp and tooth of adder
  Under leaf of rose lie.

Warned, advised in vain, abandon
  Warning and advice too,
Let the child lay wilful hand on
  Den of cockatrice too.

I, thy servant, or thy master,
  One or both—no matter;
If the former—firmer, faster,
  Surer, still the latter.
Lull thee, soothe thee, with my singing,
  Bid thee sleep, and ponder
On my lullabies, still ringing
  Through thy dreamland yonder.

SCENE—A WOODED RISING GROUND, NEAR THE RHINE. HUGO *and*
  AGATHA *resting under the trees.* THURSTON, EUSTACE, *and*
  followers, a little apart. ORION. *(Noonday.) The Towers of*
  the Convent in the distance.

AGATHA :

I sit on the greensward, and hear the bird sing,
'Mid the thickets where scarlet and white blos-
  soms cling ;
And beyond the sweet uplands all golden with
  flower,
It looms in the distance, the grey convent tower.
And the emerald earth and the sapphire-hued sky
Keep telling me ever my spring has gone by ;
Ah ! spring premature, they are tolling thy knell,
In the wind's soft adieu, in the bird's sweet farewell.
Oh ! why is the greensward with garlands so gay,
That I quail at the sight of my prison-house grey ?
Oh ! why is the bird's note so joyous and clear ?
The caged bird must pine in a cage doubly drear.

HUGO :

May the lances of Dagobert harry their house,
If they coax or intimidate thee to take vows ;
May the freebooters pillage their shrines, should
  they dare
To touch with their scissors thy glittering hair.

Our short and sweet journey now draws to an end,
And homeward my sorrowful way I must wend ;
Oh, fair one ! oh, loved one ! I would I were free,
To squander my life in the greenwood with thee.

ORION (*aside*) :

Ho ! seeker of knowledge, so grave and so wise,
Touch her soft curl again—look again in her eyes,
Forget for the nonce musty parchments, and learn
How the slow pulse may quicken—the cold blood
    may burn.
Ho ! fair fickle maiden, so blooming and shy,
The old love is dead, let the old promise die !
Thou dost well, thou dost wise, take the word of
    Orion,
" A living dog always before a dead lion !"

   .   .   .   .   .   .

THURSTON :

Ye varlets, I would I knew which of ye burst
Our wine-skin—what, ho ! must I perish with
   . thirst ?
Go, Henry, thou hast a glib tongue, go and ask
Thy lord to send Ralph to yon inn for a flask.

HENRY :

Nay, Thurston, not so ; I decline to disturb
Our lord for the present ; go thou, or else curb
Thy thirst, or drink water, as I do.

THURSTON :

                      Thou knave
Of a page, dost thou wish me the cholic to have ?

ORION (*aside*) :

That clown is a thoroughbred Saxon. He thinks
With pleasure on nought save hard blows and
    strong drinks ;
In hell he will scarce go athirst if once given
An inkling of any good liquors in heaven.

   .   .   .   .   .   .

Hugo :

Our Pontiff to manhood at Engelmehr grew,
The priests there are many, the nuns are but few.
I love not the Abbot—'tis needless to tell
My reason ; but all of the Abbess speak well.

Agatha :

Through vineyards and cornfields beneath us, the
    Rhine
Spreads and winds, silver-white, in the merry sun-
    shine ;
And the air, overcharged with a subtle perfume,
Grows faint from the essence of manifold bloom.

Hugo :

And the tinkling of bells, and the bleating of sheep,
And the chaunt from the fields, where the labourers
    reap
The earlier harvest, comes faint on the breeze
That whispers so faintly in hedgerows and trees.

Orion :

And a waggon wends slow to those turrets and spires,
To feed the fat monks and the corpulent friars ;
It carries the corn, and the oil, and the wine,
The honey and milk from the shores of the Rhine.
The oxen are weary and spent with their load ;
They pause, but the driver doth recklessly goad
Up yon steep, flinty rise ; they have staggered and
    reeled.
Even devils may pity dumb beasts of the field.

Agatha (sings):

> Oh ! days and years departed,
> Vain hopes, vain fears that smarted,
> I turn to you, sad-hearted—
>   I turn to you in tears !
> Your daily suns shone brightly,
> Your happy dreams came nightly,
> Flowers bloomed and birds sang lightly,
>   Through all your hopes and fears !

You halted not, nor tarried,
Your hopes have all miscarried,
And even your fears are buried,
   Since fear with hope must die
You halted not, but hasted,
And flew past, childhood wasted,
And girlhood scarcely tasted,
   Now womanhood is nigh.

Yet I forgive your wronging,
Dead seasons round me thronging,
With yearning and with longing,
   I call your bitters sweet.
Vain longing, and vain yearning,
There now is no returning:
Oh! beating heart and burning,
   Forget to burn and beat!

Oh! childish suns and showers,
Oh! girlish thorns and flowers,
Oh! fruitless days and hours,
   Oh! groundless hopes and fears:
The birds still chirp and twitter,
And still the sunbeams glitter:
Oh! barren years and bitter,
   Oh! bitter barren years!

SCENE—THE SUMMIT OF A BURNING MOUNTAIN. *Night. A terrific storm.* ORION (*undisguised*).

ORION (*sings*):

From fathomless depths of abysses
   Where fires unquenchable burst,
From the blackness of darkness, where hisses
   The brood of the serpent accurs'd;
From shrines, where the hymns are the weeping
   And wailing and gnashing of teeth,
Where the palm is the pang never-sleeping,
   Where the worm never-dying, is the wreath;
Where all fruits save wickedness wither,
   Whence nought save despair can be gleaned—
Come hither! come hither! come hither!
   Fall'n angel, fell sprite, and foul fiend.
Come hither! the bands are all broken
   And loosed, in hell's innermost womb,
When the spell unpronounceable spoken
   Divides the unspeakable gloom.

EVIL SPIRITS *approach.* *The storm increases.*

EVIL SPIRITS (*singing*) :

We hear thee, we seek thee, on pinions
  That darken the shades of the shade ;
Oh ! Prince of the Air, with dominions
  Encompass'd, with powers array'd,
With majesty cloth'd as a garment,
  Begirt with a shadowy shine,
Whose feet scorch the hill-tops that are meant
  As footstools for thee and for thine.

ORION (*sings*) :

How it swells through each pause of the thunder,
  And mounts through each lull of the gust,
Through the crashing of crags torn asunder,
  And the hurtling of trees in the dust ;
With its chorus of loud lamentations,
  With its dreary and hopeless refrain !
'Tis the cry of all tongues and all nations,
  That suffer and shudder in vain.

EVIL SPIRITS (*singing*) :

'Tis the cry of all tongues and all nations ;
  Our song shall chime in with their strain ;
Lost spirits blend their wild exultations
  With the sighing of mortals in pain.

ORION (*sings*) :

With just light enough to see sorrows
  In this world, and terrors beyond,
'Twixt the day's bitter pangs and the morrow's
  Dread doubts, to despair and despond,
Man lingers through toils unavailing
  For blessings that baffle his grasp ;
To his cradle he comes with a wailing,
  He goes to his grave with a gasp.

EVIL SPIRITS (*singing*) :

His birth is a weeping and wailing,
  His death is a groan and a gasp ;
O'er the seed of the woman prevailing,
  Thus triumphs the seed of the asp.

SCENE—CHAMBER OF A WAYSIDE INN. HUGO *sitting alone. Evening.*

HUGO :

And now the parting is over,
  The parting should end the pain ;
And the restless heart may recover,
  And so may the troubled brain.

D

I am sitting within the chamber
   Whose windows look on the porch,
Where the roses cluster and clamber;
   We halted here on our march
With her to the convent going,
   And now I go back alone;
Ye roses budding and blowing,
   Ye heed not though she is flown.

I remember the girlish gesture,
   The sportive and childlike grace,
With which she crumpled and pressed your
   Rose leaves to her rose-hued face.
Shall I think on her ways hereafter—
   On those flashes of mirth and grief,
On that April of tears and laughter,
   On our parting, bitterly brief?

I remember the bell at sunrise
   That sounded so solemnly,
Bidding monk, and prelate, and nun rise;
   I rose ere the sun was high.
Down the long, dark, dismal passage,
   To the door of her resting-place
I went, on a farewell message,
   I trod with a stealthy pace.
There was no one there to see us
   When she opened her chamber door.
" *Miserere, mei Deus,*"
   Rang faint from the convent choir.
I remember the dark and narrow
   And scantily-furnished room;
And the gleam, like a golden arrow,
   The gleam that lighted the gloom.
One couch, one seat, and one table,
   One window, and only one—

It stands in the eastern gable,
 It faces the rising sun;
One ray shot through it, and one light
 On doorway and threshold played.
She stood within in the sunlight,
 I stood without in the shade.

I remember that bright form under
 The sheen of that slanting ray.
I spoke—" For life we must sunder,
 Let us sunder without delay.
Let us sever without preamble,
 As brother and sister part,
For the sake of one pleasant ramble,
 That will live in at least one heart."
Still the choir in my ears rang faintly,
 In the distance dying away,
Sweetly and sadly and saintly,
 Through arch and corridor grey !
And thus we parted forever,
 Between the shade and the shine;
Not as brother and sister sever—
 I fondled her hands in mine.
Still the choir in my ears rang deaden'd
 And dull'd, though audible yet;
And she redden'd, and paled, and redden'd—
 Her lashes and lids grew wet.
Not as brother severs from sister,
 My lips clung fast to her lips;
She shivered and shrank when I kissed her.
 On the sunbeam drooped the eclipse.

I remember little of the parting
 With the Abbot, down by the gate,
My men were eager for starting;
 I think he press'd me to wait.

From the lands where convent and glebe lie,
   From manors, the church's right,
Where I fought temptation so feebly,
   I too felt eager for flight.

Alas ! the parting is over :
   The parting, but not the pain—
Oh ! sweet was the purple clover
   And sweet was the yellow grain ;
And sweet were the woody hollows
   On the summery Rhineward track ;
But a winter untimely swallows
   All sweets as I travel back.

Yet, I feel assured, in some fashion
   Ere the hedges are crisp with rime
I shall conquer this senseless passion,
   'Twill yield to toil and to time.
I will fetter these fancies roaming ;
   Already the sun has dipt ;
I will trim the lamps in the gloaming,
   I will finish my manuscript.
Through the night-watch, unflagging study
   Shall banish regrets perforce ;
As soon as the east is ruddy
   Our bugle shall sound " to horse ! "

SCENE—Another Wayside House, near the Norman Frontier.
   Hugo and Orion in a chamber. Evening.
ORION :
   Your eyes are hollow, your step is slow,
      And your cheek is pallid as though from toil,
   Watching or fasting, by which I know
      That you have been burning the midnight oil.

HUGO :

Ay, three nights running.

ORION :   'Twill never do

To travel all day and study all night ;

Will you join in a gallop through mist and dew,

In a flight that may vie with the eagle's flight ?

HUGO :

With all my heart.   Shall we saddle " Rollo ?"

ORION :

Nay, leave him undisturb'd in his stall ;

I have steeds he would hardly care to follow.

HUGO :

Follow, forsooth ! he can lead them all.

ORION :

Touching his merits we will not quarrel ;

But let me mount you for once, enough

Of work may await your favourite sorrel,

And the paths we must traverse to-night are
rough.

But first let me mix you a beverage,

To invigorate your enfeebled frame.

[*He mixes a draught and hands it to* HUGO.

All human ills this draught can assuage.

HUGO :

It hisses and glows like liquid flame ;

Say, what quack nostrum is this thou'st brew'd ?

Speak out ; I am learn'd in the chemist's lore.

ORION :

There is nothing but what will do you good ;

And the drugs are simples ; 'tis hellebore,

Nepenthé, upas, and dragon's blood,

Absinth, and mandrake, and mandragore.

HUGO :

I will drink it, although, by mass and rood,

I am just as wise as I was before.

SCENE—A ROUGH HILLY COUNTRY. HUGO *and* ORION, *riding at
     speed on black horses. Mountains in the distance. Night.*

HUGO :

> See, the sparks that fly from our hoof-strokes make
> A fiery track that gleams in our wake ;
> Like a dream the dim landscape past us shoots,
> Our horses fly.

ORION :   They are useful brutes,

> Though somewhat skittish ; the foam is whit'ning
> The crest and rein of my courser " Lightning,"
> He pulls to-night, being short of work,
> And takes his head with a sudden jerk ;
> Still heel and steady hand on the bit,
> For that is " Tempest" on which you sit.

HUGO :

> 'Tis the bravest steed that ever I back'd,
> Did'st mark how he cross'd yon cataract ?
> From hoof to hoof I should like to measure
> The space he clear'd.

ORION :   He can clear at leisure

> A greater distance.   Observe the chasm
> We are nearing.   Ha ! did you feel a spasm
> As we flew over it.

HUGO :   Not at all.

ORION :

> Nathless 'twas an ugly place for a fall.

HUGO :

> Let us try a race to yon mountain high
> That rears its dusky peak 'gainst the sky.

ORION :

> I won't disparage your horsemanship,
> But your steed will stand neither spur nor whip,
> And is hasty and hard to steer at times.
> We must travel far ere the midnight chimes ;

We must travel back ere the east is gray.
Ho! "Lightning" and "Tempest!" Away! Away!

> *[They ride on faster.*

SCENE—A Peak in a Mountainous Country overhanging a Rocky
Pass. Hugo *and* Orion *on black horses. Midnight.*

Hugo:

These steeds are sprung from no common race,
Their vigour seems to annihilate space :
What hast thou brought me here to see ?

Orion :

No boisterous scene of unhallow'd glee,
No sabbath of witches coarse and rude,
But a mystic and musical interlude ;
You have long'd to explore the scrolls of Fate.
Dismount as I do, and listen and wait.

> *[They dismount.*

Orion (*chanting*) :

> Spirits of earth and air and sea,
>   Spirits unclean, and spirits untrue,
> By the symbols three, that shall nameless be ;
>   One of your masters calls on you.

Spirits (*chanting in the distance*):

> From the bowels of earth, where gleams the gold ;
> From the air, where the powers of darkness hold
>   Their court ; from the white sea-foam
> Whence the white rose-tinted goddess sprung
> Whom poets of every age have sung,
>   Ever we come ! we come !

Hugo :

How close to our ears the thunder peals
How the earth beneath us shudders and reels !

A Voice (*chanting*) :

> Woe to the earth !   Where men give death !
>   And women give birth !
> To the sons of Adam, by Cain or Seth !
>   Plenty and dearth !

> To the daughters of Eve, who toil and spin,
>   Barren of worth !
> Let them sigh and sicken and suffer and sin !
>   Woe to the earth !

HUGO :

    What is yon phantom large and dim

    That over the mountain seems to swim ?

ORION :

    'Tis the scarlet woman of Babylon !

HUGO :

    Whence does she come ?   Where has she gone ?

    And who is she ?

ORION :   You would know too much ;

    There are subjects on which I dare not touch,

    And if I were to try and enlighten you

    I should probably fail, and possibly frighten you ;

    You had better ask some learned divine,

    Whose opinion is p'rhaps worth as much as mine

    In his own conceit ; and who besides

    Could tell you the brand of the beast she rides ;

    What can you see in the valley yonder ?

    Speak out ; I can hear you, for all the thunder.

HUGO :

    I see four shadowy altars rise,

    They seem to swell and dilate in size,

    Larger and clearer now they loom,

    Now, fires are lighting them through the gloom.

A VOICE (*chanting*) :

> The first a golden-hued fire shows,
> A blood red flame on the second glows,
> The blaze on the third is tinged like the rose,
> From the fourth a column of black smoke goes.

ORION :

    Can you see all this ?

HUGO :   I see and hear ;

    The lights and hues are vivid and clear.

SPIRITS (*sing at the first altar*) :

> Hail, Mammon ! while man buys and barters
>> Thy kingdom in this world is sure,
> Thy prophets thou hast and thy martyrs,
>> Great things in thy name they endure ;
> Thy fetters of gold crush the miser,
>> The usurer bends at thy shrine,
> And the wealthier nations and the wiser
>> Bow with us at this altar of thine.

SPIRITS (*sing at the second altar*) :

> Hail, Moloch ! whose banner floats blood-red
>> From pole to equator unfurl'd,
> Whose laws redly written have stood red,
>> And shall stand while standeth this world ;
> Clad in purple, with thy diadem gory,
>> Thy sceptre the blood-dripping steel,
> Thy subjects with us give thee glory,
>> With us at thine altar they kneel.

SPIRITS (*sing at the third altar*) :

> Hail, Sovereign ! whose fires are kindled
>> By sparks from the bottomless pit,
> Has thy worship diminish'd or dwindled ?
>> Do the yokes of thy slaves lightly sit ?
> Nay, the men of all climes and all races
>> Are stirr'd by the flames that now stir us ;
> Then (as we do) they fall on their faces,
>> Crying, " Hear us ! Oh ! Ashtaroth, hear us !

SPIRITS (*all in chorus*) :

> The vulture her carrion swallows,
>> Returns to his vomit the dog,
> In the slough of uncleanliness wallows
>> The he-goat and revels the hog.
> Men are wise with their schools and their teachers,
>> Men are just with their creeds and their priests ;
> Yet in spite of their pedants and their preachers
>> They backslide in footprints of beasts !

HUGO :

> From the smoky altar there seems to come
> A stifled murmur, a droning hum.

ORION :

> With that we have nothing at all to do,
> Or at least, not now, neither I nor you ;

Though some day or other, possibly,
We may see it closer, both you and I ;
Let us visit the nearest altar first ;
Whence the yellow fires flicker and burst,
Like the flames from molten ore that spring ;
We may stand in the pale of the outer ring,
But forbear to trespass within the inner
Lest the sins of the past should find out the sinner.

    [*They approach the first altar, and stand within*
       the outer circle which surrounds it, and near
       the inner.

SPIRITS (*sing*) :

> Beneath us it flashes,
>   The glittering gold,
> Though it turneth to ashes
>   And dross in the hold ;
> Yet man will endeavour,
>   By fraud or by strife,
> To grasp it and never
>   To yield it with life.

ORION :

What can you see ?

HUGO :   Some decrepid shapes
That are neither dwarfs, nor demons, nor apes,
In the hollow earth they appear to store
And rake together great heaps of ore.

ORION :

These are the gnomes, coarse sprites and rough :
Come on, of these we have seen enough.

    [*They approach second altar, and stand as before.*

SPIRITS (*singing*) :

> Above us it flashes,
>   The glittering steel,
> Though the red blood splashes
>   Where its victims reel ;
> Yet man will endeavour
>   To grapple the hilt,
> And to wield the blade ever,
>   Till his life be spilt.

ORION :

What see you now ?

HUGO :   A rocky glen,

A horrid jumble of fighting men,

And a face that somewhere I've seen before.

ORION :

Come on ; there is naught worth seeing more

Except the altar of Ashtaroth.

HUGO :

To visit that altar I am loth.

ORION :

Why so ?

HUGO :

                      Nay, I cannot fathom why ;

But I feel no curiosity.

ORION :

Come on.   Stand close to the inner ring,

And hear how sweetly these spirits sing.

                              [*They approach third altar.*

SPIRITS (*sing*) :

> Around us it flashes,
>   The cestus of one
> Born of white foam that dashes
>   Beneath the white sun ;
> Let the mortal take heart, he
>   Has nothing to dare :
> She is fair, Queen Astarté,
>   Her subjects are fair !

ORION :

What see you now, friend ?

HUGO :   Wood and wold,

And forms that look like the nymphs of old.

There is nothing here worth looking at twice.

I have seen enough.

ORION :   You are far too nice ;

Nevertheless you must look again.

Those forms will fade.

HUGO :   They are growing less plain.
They vanish.   I see a door that seems
To open ; a ray of sunlight gleams
From a window behind, a vision as fair
As the flush of dawn is standing there.

> [*He gazes earnestly.*

ORION (*sings*) :

Higher and hotter the white flames glow,
And the adamant may be thaw'd like snow,
And the life for a single chance may go,
       And the soul for a certainty.
Oh ! vain and shallow philosopher,
Dost feel them quicken, dost feel them stir,
The thoughts that have stray'd again to *her*,
       From whom thou hast sought to fly ?

Lo ! the furnace is heated till sevenfold ;
Is thy brain still calm ?   Is thy blood still cold
To the curls that wander in ripples of gold
       On the shoulders of ivory ?
Do the large dark eyes and the small red mouth
Consume thine heart with a fiery drouth,
Like the fierce sirocco that sweeps from the south,
       When the deserts are parch'd and dry ?

Aye, start and shiver and catch thy breath,
The sting is certain, the venom is death,
And the scales are flashing the fruit beneath,
       And the fang striketh suddenly.
At the core the ashes are bitter and dead,
But the rind is fair and the rind is red,
It has ever been pluck'd since the serpent said,
       Thou shalt *not surely* die.

> [HUGO *tries to enter the inner ring,* ORION *holds
> him back ; they struggle.*

HUGO :

Unhand me, slave ! or quail to the rod !
Agatha !   Speak ! in the name of God !

> [*The vision disappears, the altars vanish.* HUGO
> *falls insensible.*

SCENE—The Wayside House. Hugo *waking in his Chamber.*
Orion *unseen at first. Morning.*

HUGO :

Vanish fair and fatal vision !
  Fleeting shade of fever'd sleep,
Chiding one, whose indecision
  Waking substance fail'd to keep ;
Picture into life half starting,
  As in life once seen before,
Parting somewhat sadly, parting
  Slowly at the chamber door ;

Were my waking senses duller ?
  Have I seen with mental eye
Light and shade and warmth and colour
  Plainer than reality ?
Sunlight that on the tangled tresses
  Every ripple gilds and tips ;
Balm and bloom and breath of kisses
  Warm on dewy scarlet lips.

Dark eyes veiling half their splendour
  'Neath their lashes' darker fringe,
Dusky, dreamy, deep, and tender,
  Passing smile and passing tinge
Dimpling fast and flushing faster ;
  Ivory chin and coral cheek,
Pearly strings, by alabaster
  Neck and arms made faint and weak ;

Drooping downcast lids enduring
  Gaze of man unwillingly ;
Sudden sidelong gleams alluring,
  Partly arch and partly shy.
Do I bless or curse that beauty ?
  Am I longing, am I loth ?
Is it passion, is it duty
  That I strive with ?   One or both ?

Round about one fiery centre
    Wayward thoughts like moths revolve.
    (He sees Orion)   ·
Ha ! Orion, thou did'st enter
    Unperceived.   I pray thee solve
These two questions : firstly, tell me
    Must I strive for wrong or right ?
Secondly, what things befell me,
    Facts, or phantasies, last night ?

ORION :

First, your strife is all a sham, you
    Know as well as I which wins ;
Second, waking sins will damn you,
    Never mind your sleeping sins ;
Both your questions thus I answer,
    Listen, ere you seek or shun :
I at least am no romancer,
    What you long for may be won.
Turn again and travel Rhineward,
    Tread once more the flowery path.

HUGO :

Ay, the flowery path, that sinward
    Pointing, ends in sin and wrath.

ORION :

Songs by love-birds lightly caroll'd
    Even the just man may allure

HUGO :

To his shame ; in this wise Harold
    Sinn'd, his punishment was sure.

ORION :

Nay, the Dane was worse than you are,
    Base and pitiless to boot,
Doubtless all are bad, yet few are
    Cruel, false and dissolute.

HUGO:

>Some sins foreign to our nature
>> Seem, we take no credit when
> We escape them.

ORION : Yet the creature
>> Sin-created, lives to sin.

HUGO :

> Be it so ; come good, come evil,
>> Ride we to the Rhine again !

ORION (*aside*):

> 'Gainst the logic of the devil
>> Human logic strives in vain.

SCENE—A CAMP NEAR THE BLACK FOREST. RUDOLPH, OSRIC, DAGO-
BERT, *and followers.* ORION *disguised as one of the Free-
lances.* Mid-day.

OSRIC :

> Now by axe of Odin, and hammer of Thor,
> And by all the gods of the Viking's war,'
> I swear we have quitted our homes in vain ;
> We have nothing to look to, glory nor gain.
> Will our galley return to Norway's shore
> With heavier gold or with costlier store ?
> Will our exploits furnish the scald with a song ?
> We have travell'd too far, we have tarried too long,
> Say, captains all, is there ever a village
> For miles around that is worth the pillage ?
> Will it pay the costs of my men or yours
> To harry the homesteads of German boors ?
> Have we cause for pride in our feats of arms
> When we plunder the peasants or sack the farms ?
> I tell thee, Rudolph of Rothenstein,
> That were thy soldiers willing as mine,
> And I sole leader of this array,
> I would give Prince Otto battle this day.

Dost thou call thy followers men of war ?
Oh Dagobert ! thou whose ancestor
On the neck of the Cæsar's offspring trod,
Who was justly surnamed " The scourge of God."
Yet in flight lies safety.   Skirmish and run
To forest and fastness ; Teuton and Hun,
From the banks of the Rhine to the Danube's
        shore,
And back to the banks of the Rhine once more ;
Retreat from the face of an arméd foe,
Robbing garden and henroost where'er you go,
Let the short alliance betwixt us cease,
I and my Norsemen will go in peace !
I wot it never will suit with us
Such existence, tame and inglorious ;
I could live no worse, living single handed,
And better with half my men disbanded.

RUDOLPH :

Jarl Osric, what would'st thou have me do ?
'Gainst Otto's army our men count few ;
With one chance of victory, fight, say I !
But not when defeat is a certainty.
If Rudiger joins us with his free-lances
Our chance will be equal to many chances ;
For Rudiger is both prompt and wary,
And his men are gallant though mercenary ;
But the knave refuses to send a lance
Till half the money is paid in advance.

DAGOBERT :

May his avarice wither him like a curse !
I guess he has heard of our late reverse ;
But, Rudolph, whether he goes or stays,
There is reason in what Jarl Osric says ;
Of provisions we need a fresh supply,
And our butts and flasks are shallow dry,

My men are beginning to grumble sadly,

'Tis no wonder, since they must fare so badly.

RUDOLPH :

We have plenty of foragers out, and still

We have plenty of hungry mouths to fill ;

And moreover by some means, foul or fair,

We must raise money ; 'tis little I care,

So long as we raise it, whence it comes.

OSRIC :

Shall we sit till nightfall biting our thumbs ?

The shortest plan is ever the best ;

Has anyone here got aught to suggest ?

ORION :

The cornfields are golden that skirt the Rhine,

Fat are the oxen, strong is the wine,

In those pleasant pastures, those cellars deep,

That o'erflow with the tears that those vineyards weep ;

Is it silver you stand in need of, or gold ?

Ingot or coin ?　There is wealth untold

In the ancient convent of Englemehr ;

That is not so very far from here.

The Abbot, esteem'd a holy man,

Will hold what he has and grasp what he can ;

The cream of the soil he loves to skim,

Why not levy a contribution on him ?

DAGOBERT :

The stranger speaks well ; not far away

That convent lies ; and one summer's day

Will suffice for a horseman to reach the gate ;

The garrison soon would capitulate,

Since the arm'd retainers are next to none,

And the walls, I wot, may be quickly won.

RUDOLPH :

I kept those walls for two months and more

When they feared the riders of Melchior ;

E

That was little over three years ago.
Their Abbot is thrifty, as well I know
He haggled sorely about the price
Of our service.

DAGOBERT: Rudolph, he paid thee twice.

RUDOLPH:

Well, what of that ?   Since then I've tried
To borrow from him ; now I know he lied
When he told me he could not spare the sum
I asked.   If we to his gates should come
He could spare it though it were doubled ; and still
This war with the church, I like it ill.

OSRIC:

The creed of our fathers is well nigh dead,
And the creed of the Christian reigns in its stead ;
But the creed of the Christian, too, may die.
For your creeds or your churches what care I !
If there be plunder at Engelmehr,
Let us strike our tents and thitherward steer.

SCENE—A FARM HOUSE ON THE RHINE (*about a mile from the
Convent.*) HUGO *in chamber alone.*

Enter ERIC.

ERIC:

What, Hugo, still at the Rhine ?   I thought
You were home. You have travell'd by stages short.

HUGO (*with hesitation*):

Our homeward march was labour in vain,
We had to retrace our steps again ;
It was here or hereabouts that I lost
Some papers of value ; at any cost
I must find them : and which way lies your course ?

ERIC:

I go to recruit Prince Otto's force.
I cannot study as you do ; I
Am wearied with inactivity,

So I carry a blade engrim'd with rust
(That a hand sloth-slacken'd has, I trust,
Not quite forgotten the way to wield)
To strike once more on the tented field.

HUGO :

Fighting is all a mistake, friend Eric,
And has been so since the age Homeric,
When Greece was shaken and Troy undone
Ten thousand lives for a worthless one.
Yet I blame you not; you might well do worse ;
Better fight and perish than live to curse
The day you were born ; and such has been
The lot of many, and shall, I ween,
Be the lot of more.   If Thurston chooses
He may go with you ; the blockhead abuses
Me and the life I lead.

Enter ORION.

ORION :   Great news !

The Engelmehr monks will shake in their shoes ;
In the soles of their callous feet will shake
The bare-footed friars.   The nuns will quake.

HUGO :

Wherefore ?

ORION :   The outlaw of Rothenstein
Has come with his soldiers to the Rhine,
Back'd by those hardy adventurers
From the northern forests of pines and firs,
And Dagobert's horse.   They march as straight
As the eagle's swoops, to the convent gate.

HUGO :

We must do something to save the place.

ORION :

They are sure to take it in any case,
Unless the sum that they ask is paid.

ERIC:

    Some effort on our part must be made.

HUGO:

    'Tis not so much for the monks I care.

ERIC:

    Nor I; but the Abbess **and** Nuns are there.

ORION:

    'Tis not our business; what can we do

    They are too many, and we are too few:

    And yet I suppose you will save if you can

    That lady, your ward or your kinswoman.

HUGO:

    She is no kinswoman of mine.

    How far is Otto's camp from the Rhine?

ORION:

    Too far for help in such time of need

    To be brought, though you used your utmost speed.

ERIC:

    Nay, that I doubt.

HUGO: And how many men

    Have they?

ORION: To your one they could muster ten.

ERIC:

    I know Count Rudolph, and terms may be made

    With him, I fancy; for though his trade

    Is a rough one now, gainsay it who can,

    He was once a knight and a gentleman.

    And Dagobert, the chief of the Huns,

    Bad as he is, will spare the nuns;

    Though neither he nor the Count could check

    Those lawless men, should they storm and sack

    The convent. Jarl Osric, too, I know,

    He is rather a formidable foe,

    And will likely enough be troublesome;

    But the others, I trust, to terms will come.

HUGO:

    Eric, how many men have you?

    I can count a score.

ERIC: I have only two.

HUGO:

    At every hazard we must try to save

    The nuns.

ERIC: Count Rudolph shall think we have

    A force that almost equals his own,

    If I can confer with him alone.

ORION:

    He is close at hand; by this time he waits

    The Abbot's reply at the convent gates.

HUGO:

    We had better send him a herald.

ERIC: Nay,

    I will go myself.   [ERIC *goes out.*

HUGO: Orion, stay!

    So this is the reed on which I've leaned,

        These are the hopes thou hast fostered, these

    The flames thou hast fanned.   Oh, lying fiend!

        Is it thus thou dost keep thy promises?

ORION:

    Strong language, Hugo, and most unjust;

        You will cry out before you are hurt—

    You will live to recall your words, I trust.

    Fear nothing from Osric or Dagobert,

    These are your friends, if you only knew it,

        And would take the advice of a friend sincere:

    Neglect his counsels and you must rue it,

        For I know by a sign the crisis is near.

    Accept the terms of these outlaws all,

        And be thankful that things have fallen out

    Exactly as you would have had them fall—

        You may save the one that you care about;

Otherwise, how did you hope to gain
    Access to her—on what pretence ?
What were the schemes that worried your brain
    To tempt her there or to lure her thence ?
You must have bungled, and raised a scandal
    About your ears, that might well have shamed
The rudest Hun, the veriest Vandal,
    Long or ever the bird was tamed.

HUGO :

The convent is scarce surrounded yet,
    We might reach and hold it against their force
Till another sun has risen and set ;
    And should I despatch my fleetest horse
To Otto—

ORION :

            For Abbot, or Monk, or Friar,
    Between ourselves 'tis little you care
If their halls are harried by steel and fire,
    Their avarice left your heritage bare.
Forsake them ! Mitres, and cowls, and hoods,
    Will cover vices while earth endures ;
Through the green and gold of the summer woods
    Ride out, with that pretty bird of yours.
If again you fail to improve your chance,
    Why, then, my friend, I can only say
You are duller far than the dullest lance
    That rides in Dagobert's troop this day.
" *Fœmina semper*," frown not thus,
    The girl was always giddy and wild ;
Vain, and foolish, and frivolous,
    Since she fled from her father's halls, a child.
I sought to initiate you once
    In the mystic lore of the old Chaldæan ;
But I found you far too stubborn a dunce,
    And your tastes are coarser and more plebeian ;

Yet mark my words, for I read the stars,
　　And trace the future in yonder sky,
To the right are wars and rumours of wars,
　　To the left are peace and prosperity.
Fear nought.　The world shall never detect
　　The cloven hoof, so carefully hid
By the scholar so staid and circumspect,
　　So wise for once, to do as he's bid.
Remember, what pangs come year by year
　　For opportunity that has fled ;
And Thora in ignorance.

Hugo :　　　　　　　　　　Name not her !
　　I am sorely tempted to strike thee dead !

Orion :
　　Nay, I hardly think you will take my life.
　　The angel Michael was once my foe ;
　　He had a little the best of our strife,
　　　　Yet he never could deal so stark a blow.

———

SCENE—A Chamber in the Nuns' Apartments of the Convent.
Agatha *and* Ursula.

Agatha :
　　My sire in my childhood pledged my hand
　　　　To Hugo—I know not why—
　　They were comrades then 'neath the Duke's com-
　　　　　　mand,
　　　　In the wars of Lombardy.
　　I thought, 'ere my summers had turned sixteen,
　　　　That mine was a grievous case ;
　　Save once, for an hour, I had never seen
　　　　My intended bridegroom's face ;
　　And maidens, vows of their own will plight.
　　　　Unknown to my kinsfolk all
　　My love was vowed to a Danish knight,
　　　　A guest in my father's hall ;

His foot fell lightest in merry dance,
　His shaft never missed the deer ;
He could fly a hawk, he could wield a lance,
　Our wildest colt he could steer.
His deep voice ringing through hall or glen
　Had never its match in song,
And little was known of his past life then,
　Or of Dorothea's wrong.
I loved him—Lady Abbess, I know
　That my love was foolish now ;
I was but a child five years ago,
　And thoughtless as bird on bough.
One evening Hugo the Norman came,
　And, to shorten a weary tale,
I fled that night (let me bear the blame),
　With Harold, by down and dale.
He had mounted me on a dappled steed,
　And another of coal-black hue
He rode himself ; and away at speed
　We fled, through the mist and dew.

Of miles we had ridden some half a score,
　We had halted beside a spring,
When the breeze to our ears through the still
　　night bore
　A distant trample and ring ;
We listen'd one breathing space, and caught
　The clatter of mounted men.
With vigour renew'd by their respite short
　Our horses dash'd through the glen.
Another league, and we listen'd in vain ;
　The breeze to our ears came mute,
But we heard them again, on the spacious plain,
　Faint tidings of hot pursuit
In the misty light of a moon half hid
　By the dark or fleecy rack,

Our shadows over the moorland slid;
   Still listening and looking back.
So we fled (with a cheering word to say
   At times as we hurried on),
From sounds that at intervals died away,
   And at intervals came anon.

Another league, and my lips grew dumb,
   And I felt my spirit quailing,
For closer those sounds began to come,
   And the speed of my horse was failing.
" The grey is weary and lame to boot,"
   Quoth Harold; "the black is strong,
And their steeds are blown with their fierce pursuit,
   What wonder! our start was long.
Now, lady, behind me mount the black,
   The double load he can bear;
We are safe when we reach the forest track,
   Fresh horses and friends wait there."
Then I sat behind him and held his waist;
   And faster we seem'd to go
By moss and moor; but for all our haste
   Came the tramp of the nearing foe;
A dyke through the mist before us hover'd:
   And, quicken'd by voice and heel,
The black overleap'd it, stagger'd, recover'd;
   Still nearer that muffled peal,
And louder on sward the hoof-strokes grew,
   And duller, though not less nigh,
On deader sand; and a dark speck drew
   On my vision suddenly,
And a single horseman in fleet career,
   Like a shadow appear'd to glide
To within six lances' lengths of our rear,
   And there for a space to bide;

Quoth Harold, " Speak, has the moon reveal'd
   His face ?"   I replied, " Not so ;
Yet 'tis none of my kinsfolk," then he wheel'd
   In the saddle and scann'd the foe,
And mutter'd, still gazing in our wake,
   " 'Tis he ; now I will not fight
The brother again, for the sister's sake
   While I can escape by flight."
" Who, Harold ?" I ask'd ; but he never spoke.
   By the cry of the bittern harsh,
And the bullfrog's dull discordant croak,
   I guess'd that we near'd the marsh,
And the moonbeam flash'd on watery sedge
   As it broke from a strip of cloud
Ragged and jagged about the edge
   And shaped like a dead man's shroud ;
And flagg'd and falter'd our gallant steed
   'Neath the weight of his double burden,
As we splash'd through water and crash'd through
     reed ;
   Then the soil began to harden,
And again we gain'd, or we seem'd to gain,
   With our foe in the deep morass,
But those fleet hoofs thunder'd, and gain'd again,
   When they trampled the firmer grass,
And I cried, and Harold again look'd back,
   And bade me fasten mine eyes on
The forest that loom'd like a patch of black
   Standing out from the faint horizon.

" Courage, sweetheart ! we are saved," he said ;
   " With the moorland our danger ends,
And close to the borders of yonder glade
   They tarry, our trusty friends."
Where the mossy uplands rise and dip .
   On the edge of the leafy dell,

With a lurch, like the lurch of a sinking ship,
    The black horse toppled and fell ;
Unharm'd we lit on the velvet sward,
    And even as I lit I lay,
But Harold uprose, unsheath'd his sword,
    And toss'd his scabbard away,
And spake through his teeth, " Good brother-in-law,
    Forbearance, at last, is spent ;
The strife that thy soul hath lusted for,
    Thou shalt have to thy soul's content !"
While he spoke, our pursuer past us swept
    Ere he rein'd his warhorse proud
To his haunches flung, then to earth he leapt,
    And my lover's voice rang loud,
" Thrice welcome ! Hugo of Normandy,
    Thou hast come at our time of need,
This lady will thank thee, so will I,
    For the loan of thy sorrel steed !"

And never a word Lord Hugo said,
    They closed 'twixt the wood and wold,
And the white steel flicker'd over my head
    In the moonlight calm and cold ;
'Mid the feathery grasses crouching low,
    With face bow'd down to the dust,
I hear'd the clash of each warded blow,
    The click of each parried thrust,
And the shuffling feet that bruis'd the lawn
    As they traversed here and there,
And the breath through the clench'd teeth heavily
      drawn,
    When breath there was none to spare ;
Sharp ringing sword-play, dull trampling heel,
    Short pause, spent force to regain,
Quick muffled footfall, harsh grating steel,
    Sharp ringing rally again,

They seem'd long hours those moments fleet
   As I counted them one by one,
Till a dead weight toppled across my feet,
   And I knew that the strife was done.

When I look'd up, after a little space,
   As though from a fearful dream,
The moon was flinging on Harold's face
   A white and a weird-like gleam;
And I felt mine ankles moist and warm
   With the blood that trickled slow
From a spot on the doublet beneath his arm,
   From a ghastly gash on his brow;
I heard the tread of the sorrel's hoof
   As he bore his lord away;
They pass'd me slowly, keeping aloof
   Like spectres misty and grey.
I thought Lord Hugo had left me there
   To die, but it was not so;
Yet then, for death I had little care,
   My soul seem'd numb'd by the blow;
A faintness follow'd, a sickly swoon,
   A long and a dreamless sleep,
And I woke to the light of a sultry noon
   In my father's castle'd keep.

And thus, Lady Abbess, it came to pass
   That my father vow'd his vow;
Must his daughter espouse the church ?   Alas!
   Is she better or wiser now ?
For some are feeble and others strong,
   And feeble am I and frail.
Mother ! 'tis not that I love the wrong,
   'Tis not that I loathe the veil,
But with heart still ready to go astray
   If assail'd by a fresh temptation,

I could sin again as I sinn'd that day
  For a girl's infatuation.
See ! Harold the Dane thou say'st is dead,
  Yet I weep *not bitterly ;*
As I fled with the Dane, so I might have fled
  With Hugo of Normandy.

URSULA :

My child, I advise no hasty vows,
  Yet I pray that in life's brief span
Thou may'st learn that our church is a fairer spouse
  Than fickle and erring man ;
Though fenced for a time by the church's pale,
  When that time expires thou 'rt free,
And we cannot force thee to take the veil,
  Nay, we scarce can counsel thee.

Enter the ABBOT *hastily.*

BASIL (*the Abbot*) :

I am sorely stricken with shame and grief,
  It has come by the selfsame sign,
A summons brief from the outlaw'd chief,
  Count Rudolph of Rothenstein.
Lady Abbess, ere worse things come to pass
  I would speak with thee alone ;
Alack and alas ! for by the rood and mass
  I fear we are all undone.

SCENE—A FARM HOUSE NEAR THE CONVENT. *A Chamber furnished with writing materials.* HUGO, ERIC, *and* THURSTON, *on one side, on the other* OSRIC, RUDOLPH, *and* DAGOBERT.

OSRIC :

We have granted too much, ye ask for more ;
I am not skilled in your clerkly lore,
I scorn your logic ; I had rather die
Than live like Hugo of Normandy ;

I am a Norseman, frank and plain ;
Ye must read the parchment over again.

ERIC :

Jarl Osric, twice we have read this scroll.

OSRIC :

Thou hast read a part.

ERIC :   I have read the whole.

OSRIC :

Ay, since I attached my signature!

ERIC :

Before and since !

RUDOLPH :

                       Nay, of this be sure,
Thou hast signed ; in fairness now let it rest.

OSRIC :

I had rather have sign'd upon Hugo's crest ;
He has argued the question mouth to mouth
With the wordy lore of the subtle south ;
Let him or any one of his band
Come and argue the question hand to hand,
With the aid of my battleaxe I will show
That a score of words are not worth one blow.

THURSTON :

To the devil with thee and thy battleaxe ;
I would send the pair of ye back in your tracks,
With an answer that even to thy boorish brain
Would scarce need repetition again.

OSRIC :

Thou Saxon slave to a milksop knight,
I will give thy body to raven and kite.

THURSTON :

Thou liest ; I am a freeborn man,
And thy huge carcass—in cubit and span
Like the giant's of Gath—'neath Saxon steel,
Shall furnish the kites with a fatter meal.

Osric :

Now, by Odin !

Rudolph : Jarl Osric, curb thy wrath ;

Our names are sign'd, our words have gone forth.

Hugo :

I blame thee, Thurston.

Thurston : And I too blame

Myself, since I follow a knight so tame !

[Thurston *goes out.*

Osric :

The Saxon hound, he said I lied !

Rudolph :

I pray thee, good Viking, be pacified.

Osric :

Why do we grant the terms they ask ?

To crush them all were an easy task.

Dagobert :

That know'st thou not ; if it come to war,

They are stronger perhaps than we bargain for.

Eric :

Jarl Osric, thou may'st recall thy words—

Should we meet again.

Osric : Should we meet with swords

Thou, too, may'st recall them to thy sorrow.

Hugo :

Eric ! we dally. Sir Count, good morrow.

SCENE—The Guest Chamber of the Convent. Hugo, Eric,
and Orion.

Eric :

Hugo, their siege we might have tried ;

This place would be easier fortified

Than I thought at first ; it is now too late,

They have cut off our access to the gate.

HUGO :

> I have weigh'd the chances and counted the cost,
> And I know by the stars that all is lost
> If we take up this quarrel.

ERIC :   So let it be !

> I yield to one who is wiser than me.   (*Aside*)
> Nevertheless, I have seen the day   ·
> When the stars would scarcely have bade us stay.

Enter the ABBOT, CYRIL, *and other monks.*

HUGO :

> Lord Abbot, we greet thee.   Good fathers all
> We bring you greeting.

ORION (*aside*) :   And comfort small.

ABBOT :

> God's benediction on˜you, my sons.

HUGO :

> May he save you, too, from Norsemen and Huns !
> Since gates are beleaguer'd and walls begirt
> By the forces of Osric and Dagobert;
> 'Tis a heavy price that the knaves demand.

ABBOT :

> Were we to mortgage the church's land
> We never could raise what they would extort.

ORION (*aside*) :

> The price is too long and the notice too short.

ERIC :

> And you know the stern alternative.

ABBOT :

> If we die we die, if we live we live ;
> God's will be done; and our trust is sure
> In Him, though his chast'nings we endure.
> Two messengers rode from here last night,
> To Otto they carry news of our plight,
> On my swiftest horses I saw them go.

ORION (*aside*) :

> Then his swiftest horses are wondrous slow.

ERIC:

> One of these is captive and badly hurt;
> By the reckless riders of Dagobert
> He was overtaken and well nigh slain,
> Not a league from here on the open plain.

ABBOT:

> But the other escap'd.

ERIC: It may be so;

> We had no word of him, but we know
> That unless you can keep these walls for a day
> At least, the Prince is too far away
> To afford relief.

ABBOT: Then a hopeless case

> Is ours, and with death we are face to face.

ERIC:

> You have arm'd retainers.

CYRIL (a Monk):   Aye, some half score;

> And some few of the brethren, less or more,
> Have in youth the brunt of the battle bided,
> Yet our armoury is but ill provided.

HUGO:

> We have terms of truce from the robbers in chief,
> Though the terms are partial, the truce but brief;
> To abbess, to nuns, and novices all,
> And to every woman within your wall
> We can offer escort, and they shall ride
> From hence in safety whate'er betide.

ABBOT:

> What escort, Hugo, can'st thou afford?

HUGO:

> Some score of riders who call me lord
> Bide at the farm not a mile from here,
> Till we rejoin them they will not stir;
> My page and armourer wait below,
> And all our movements are watch'd by the foe.

F

Strict stipulation was made, of course,
That except ourselves, neither man nor horse
Should enter your gates—they were keen to shun
The chance of increasing your garrison.

ERIC :

I hold safe conduct here in my hand,
Signed by the chiefs of that lawless band ;
See Rudolph's name, no disgrace to a clerk,
And Dagobert's scrawl, and Osric's mark ;
Jarl sign'd sorely against his will,
With a scratch like the print of a raven's bill ;
But the foe have muster'd in sight of the gate,
For another hour they will scarcely wait ;
Bid abbess and dames prepare with haste,
We have neither moments nor words to waste.

HUGO :

Lord Abbot, I tell thee candidly
There is no great love between thou and I,
As well thou know'st ; and nevertheless
I would we were more, or thy foes were less.

ABBOT :

I will summon the Lady Abbess straight.

ERIC :   [*The* ABBOT *and Monks go out.*
'Tis hard to leave these men to their fate,
Norseman and Hun will never relent :
Their day of grace upon earth is spent.

                    [HUGO *goes out, followed by* ORION.

SCENE—THE CORRIDOR OUTSIDE THE GUEST CHAMBER.   HUGO
    pacing up and down, ORION *leaning against the wall.*

HUGO :

My day of grace with theirs is past.
    I might have saved them ; 'tis too late—
Too late for both.   The die is cast,
    And I resign me to my fate.
        God's vengeance I await.

ORION:

> The boundary 'twixt right and wrong
>   Is not so easy to discern,
> And man is weak and fate is strong,
>   And destiny man's hopes will spurn,
>   Man's schemes will overturn.

HUGO:

> Thou liest, thou fiend! Not unawares
>   The sinner swallows Satan's bait,
> Nor pits conceal'd nor hidden snares
>   Seeks blindly; wherefore dost thou prate
>   Of destiny and fate?

ORION:

> Who first named fate? But never mind,
>   Let that pass by—to Adam's fall
> And Adam's curse look back, and find
>   Iniquity the lot of all
>   And sin original.

HUGO:

> But I have sinn'd, repented, sinn'd
>   Till seven times that sin may be
> By seventy multiplied; the wind
>   Is constant when compared with me,
>   And stable is the sea!

> My hopes are sacrificed, for what?
>   For days of folly, less or more,
> For years to see those dead hopes rot
>   Like dead weeds scatter'd on the shore
>   Beyond the surfs that roar!

ORION:

> The wiles of Eve are swift to smite;
>   Ay, swift to smite and not to spare—
> Red lips and round limbs sweet and white,
>   Dark eyes and sunny silken hair,
>   Thy betters may ensnare.

HUGO:

> Not so; the strife 'twixt hell and heaven
> I felt last night, and well I knew
> The crisis; but my aid was given
> To hell. Thou'st known the crisis too,
> For once thou'st spoken true
>
> Having foretold it; there remains
> For grace no time, for hope no room;
> Even now I seem to feel the pains
> Of hell, that wait beyond the gloom
> Of my dishonour'd tomb.
>
> Thou who hast lived and died to save
> Us sinners, Christ of Galilee!
> Thy great love pardon'd and forgave
> The dying thief upon the tree,
> Thou can'st not pardon me!
>
> Dear Lord! hear thou my latest prayer,
> For prayer must die since hope is dead;
> Thy Father's vengeance let me bear,
> Nor let my guilt be visited
> Upon a guiltless head!
>
> Ah! God is just! Full sure I am
> He never did predestinate
> Our souls to hell. Ourselves we damn—
> (*To* ORION, *with sudden passion*)
> Serpent! I know thee now, too late;
> Curse thee! Work out thy hate!

ORION:

> I hate thee not, thy grievous plight
> Would move my pity, but I bear
> A curse to which thy curse seems light;
> Thy wrong is better than my right,
> My day is darker than thy night;
> Beside the whitest hope I share
> How white is thy despair!

SCENE—The Chapel of the Convent. Ursula, Agatha, *Nuns and Novices.*

(Hymn of the Nuns) :

> Jehovah ! we bless thee,
>> All works of thine hand
> Extol thee, confess thee,
>> By sea and by land,
> By mountain and river,
>> By forest and glen,
> They praise thee for ever !
>> And ever ! Amen !

> The heathen are raging
>> Against thee, oh Lord !
> The ungodly are waging
>> Rash war against God !
> Arise, and deliver
>> Us, sheep of thy pen,
> Who praise thee for ever !
>> And ever ! Amen !

> Thou, shepherd of Zion !
>> Thy firstlings did'st tear
> From jaws of the lion,
>> From teeth of the bear ;
> Thy strength to deliver
>> Is strong now as then.
> We praise thee for ever !
>> And ever ! Amen !

> Thine arm hath deliver'd
>> Thy servants of old,
> Hath scatter'd and shiver'd
>> The spears of the bold,
> Hath emptied the quiver
>> Of bloodthirsty men.
> We praise thee for ever !
>> And ever ! Amen !

> Nathless shall thy right hand
>> Those counsels fulfil,
> Most wise in thy sight, and
>> We bow to thy will ;
> Thy children quail never
>> For dungeon or den,
> They praise thee for ever !
>> And ever ! Amen !

Though fierce tribulation
        Endure for a space,
Yet, God ! our salvation !
        We gain by thy grace
At end of life's fever,
        Bliss passing man's ken ;
There to praise thee for ever !
        And ever !   Amen ;

SCENE—The Guest Room of the Convent. Hugo, Eric, and
        Orion.   *Enter* Ursula, Agatha, *and Nuns.*

URSULA :

Hugo ! we reject thine offers,
    Not that we can buy
Safety from the church's coffers,
    Neither can we fly.
Far too great the price they seek is,
    Let their lawless throng
Come, we wait their coming ; weak is
    Man, but God is strong.

ERIC :

Think again on our proposals,
    It will be too late
When the robbers hold carousals
    On this side the gate.

URSULA :

For myself I speak and others
    Weak and frail as I,
We will not desert our brothers
    In adversity.

HUGO (*to the Nuns*) :

Does the Abbess thus advance her
    Will before ye all ?

A NUN :

We will stay.

HUGO :   Is this thine answer,
    Agatha ?   The wall

Is a poor protection truly,
   And the gates are weak,
And the Norsemen most unruly.
   Come, then.

A NUN (*to* AGATHA):   Sister, speak !

ORION (*aside to* HUGO):

Press her !   She her fears dissembling,
   Stands irresolute ;
She will yield—her limbs are trembling,
   Though her lips are mute.

              [*A trumpet is heard without.*

ERIC :

Hark ! their savage war-horn blowing
   Chafes at our delay.

HUGO :

Agatha, we must be going.
   Come, girl !

AGATHA (*clinging to* URSULA):   Must I stay ?

URSULA :

Nay, my child, thou shalt not make me
   Judge : I cannot give
Orders to a novice.

AGATHA :   Take me,
   Hugo !   Let me live !

ERIC (*to Nuns*) :

Foolish women ! will ye tarry,
   Spite of all we say ?

HUGO :

Must we use our strength and carry
   You by force away ?

URSULA :

Bad enough thou art, Sir Norman,
   Yet thou wilt not do
This thing.   Shame !—on men make war, man,
   Not on women few.

ERIC :

 Heed her not—her life she barters
  Of her free accord,
 For her faith ; and, doubtless, martyrs
  Have their own reward.

URSULA :

 In the Church's cause thy father
  Never grudged his blade—
 Hugo, did he rue it ?

ORION :   Rather !

 He was poorly paid.

HUGO :

 Abbess, this is not my doing,
  I have said my say ;
 How can I avert the ruin,
  Even for a day ?
 Since they count two hundred fairly,
  While we count a score ;
 And thine own retainers barely
  Count a dozen more.

AGATHA (*kneeling to* URSULA) :

 Ah ! forgive me, Lady Abbess,
  Bless me ere I go ;
 She who under sod and slab is
  Lying cold and low
 Scarce would turn away in anger
  From a child so frail ;
 Not dear life, but deadly danger
  Makes her daughter quail.

HUGO :

 Eric, will those faces tearful
  To God's judgment seat
 Haunt us ?

ERIC :   Death is not so fearful.

HUGO :   No, but life is sweet,

 Sweet, for once, to me, though sinful.

ORION (*to* HUGO):   Earth is scant of bliss ;
   Wisest he who takes his skin-full,
     When the chance is his.
  (*To* URSULA):
   Lady Abbess ! stay and welcome
     Osric's savage crew ;
   Yet when pains of death and hell come,
     Thou thy choice may'st rue.
URSULA (*to* ORION):
   What do'st thou 'neath roof trees sacred ?
     Man or fiend, depart !   .
ORION :
   Dame, thy tongue is sharp and acrid,
     Yet I bear the smart.
URSULA (*advancing, and raising up a crucifix*):
   I conjure thee by this symbol
     Leave us !
                   [ORION *goes out hastily.*
HUGO :   Ha ! the knave,
   He has made an exit nimble :
     Abbess ! thou art brave.
   Yet once gone, we're past recalling ;
     Let no blame be mine.
   See, thy sisters' tears are falling
     Fast, and so are thine.
URSULA :
   Fare you well !   The teardrop splashes
     Vainly on the ice.
   Ye will sorrow o'er our ashes
     And your cowardice.
ERIC :
   Sorry am I, yet my sorrow
     Cannot alter fate ;
   Should Prince Otto come to-morrow,
     He will come too late.

HUGO :

    Nay, old comrade, she hath spoken
      Words we must not hear,
    Shall we pause for sign or token—
      Taunted twice with fear ?
    Yonder, hilt to hilt adjusted,
    Stand the swords in which we trusted
    Years ago.   Their blades have rusted,
      So, perchance, have we.
    Ursula ! thy words may shame us,
    Yet we once were counted famous,
    Morituri, salutamus,
      Aut victuri, te !   *[They go out.*

SCENE—THE OUTSKIRTS OF RUDOLPH'S CAMP. RUDOLPH, OSRIC,
        and DAGOBERT. HUGO.

RUDOLPH :

    Lord Hugo ! thy speech is madness ;
      Thou hast tax'd our patience too far :
    We offer'd thee peace—with gladness,
      We gladly accept thy war.

DAGOBERT :

    And the clemency we extended
      To thee and thine, we recall ;
    And the treaty 'twixt us is ended—
      We are ready to storm the wall.

OSRIC :

    Now tear yon parchment to tatters,
      Thou shalt make no further use
    Of our safeguard : the wind that scatters
      The scroll shall scatter the truce.

HUGO :

    Jarl Osric, to save the spilling
      Of blood and the waste of life,
    I am willing, if thou art willing,
      With thee to decide this strife ;

Let thy comrades draw their force back :
  I defy thee to single fight,
I will meet thee on foot or horseback,
  And God shall defend the right.

RUDOLPH :
No single combat shall settle
  This strife : thou art over bold—
Thou hast put us all on our mettle,
  Now the game in our hands we hold.

DAGOBERT :
Our lances round thee have hover'd,
  Have seen where thy fellows bide ;
Thy weakness we have discover'd,
  Thy nakedness we have spied.

OSRIC :
And hearken, knight, to my story—
  When sack'd are the convent shrines,
When the convent thresholds are gory,
  And quaff'd are the convent wines ;
When our beasts with pillage are laden,
  And the clouds of our black smoke rise
From yon tower : one fair-haired maiden
  Is singled as Osric's prize.
I will fit her with chain and collar
  Of red gold, studded with pearls,
With bracelet of gold, Sir Scholar :
  The queen of my captive girls.

HUGO (*savagely*) :
May the Most High God of battles,
  The Lord and Ruler of fights,
Who breaketh the shield that rattles,
  Who snappeth the sword that smites,
In whose hands are footman and horseman
  At whose breath they conquer or flee,
Never show me his mercy, Norseman !
  If I show mercy to thee.

OSRIC :

>What ho ! art thou drunk, Sir Norman ?
>Has the wine made thy pale cheek red ?
>Now, I swear by Odin and Thor, man,
>Already I count thee dead.

RUDOLPH :

>I crave thy pardon for baulking
>The flood of thine eloquence,
>But thou can'st not scare us with talking,
>I therefore pray thee, go hence.

OSRIC :

>Though I may not take up thy guantlet,
>Should we meet where the steel strikes fire,
>'Twixt thy casque and thy charger's frontlet
>The choice will perplex thy squire.

HUGO :

>When the Norman rowels are goading,
>When glitters the Norman glaive,
>Thou shalt call upon Thor and Odin :
>They shall not hear thee nor save.
>" Should we meet !" Ay, the chance may fall so,
>In the furious battle drive,
>So may God deal with me—more, also !
>If we separate, both alive !

SCENE—THE COURT-YARD OF THE OLD FARM. EUSTACE *and other followers of* HUGO *and* ERIC *lounging about. Enter* THURSTON *hastily, with swords under his arm.*

THURSTON :

>Now saddle your horses and girth them tight,
>And see that your weapons are sharp and bright.
>Come, lads, get ready as fast as you can.

EUSTACE :

>Why, what's this bustle about, old man ?

THURSTON :

> Well, it seems Lord Hugo has changed his mind,
> As the weathercock veers with the shifting wind;
> He has gone in person to Osric's camp,
> To tell him to pack up his tents and tramp :
> But I guess he won't.

EUSTACE :   Then I hope he will.

> They are plenty to eat us, as well as to kill.

RALPH :

> And I hope he won't—I begin to feel
> A longing to moisten my thirsty steel.
>
> > [*They begin to saddle and make preparations*
> > *for a skirmish.*

THURSTON :

> I've a couple of blades to look to here.
> In their scabbards I scarcely could make them stir
> At first, but I'll sharpen them both ere long.

A MAN-AT-ARMS :

> Hurrah for a skirmish !   Who'll give us a song ?

THURSTON (*sings, cleaning and sharpening*) :

> > Hurrah for the sword !   I hold one here,
> >   And I scour at the rust, and say
> > 'Tis the umpire, this, and the arbiter
> >   That settles in the fairest way ;
> > For it stays false tongues and it cools hot blood,
> >   And it lowers the proud one's crest ;
> > And the law of the land is sometimes good,
> >   But the law of the sword is best.
> > In all disputes 'tis the shortest plan,
> >   The surest and best appeal ;—
> > What else can decide between man and man ?

(*Chorus of all*) : ·

> > Hurrah ! for the bright blue steel !

THURSTON (*sings*) :

> > Hurrah ! for the sword of Hugo our lord !
> >   'Tis a trusty friend and a true ;
> > It has held its own on a grassy sward,
> >   When its blade shone bright and blue.

Though it never has stricken in anger hard,
    And has scarcely been cleansed from rust,
Since the day when it broke through Harold's guard
    With our favourite cut and thrust ;
Yet Osric's crown will look somewhat red,
    And his brain will be apt to reel,
Should the trenchant blade come down on his head—

(Chorus of all) :

    Hurrah ! for the bright blue steel !

THURSTON *(sings)* :

    Hurrah ! for the sword of our ally bold,
        It has done good service to him ;
    It has held its own on an open wold,
        When its edge was in keener trim.
    It may baffle the plots of the wisest skull,
        It may slacken the strongest limb,
    Make the brains full of forethought void and null,
        And the eyes full of farsight, dim ;
    And the hasty hands are content to wait,
        And the knees are compell'd to kneel,
    Where it falls with the weight of a downstroke straight,

(Chorus of all) :

    Hurrah ! for the bright blue steel !

THURSTON *(sings)* :

    Hurrah ! for the sword—I've one of my own :
        And I think I may safely say,
    Give my enemy his, let us stand alone,
        And our quarrel shall end one way ;
    One way or the other—it matters not much,
        So the question be fairly tried.
    Oh ! peacemaker good, bringing peace with a touch,
        Thy clients will be satisfied.
    As a judge, thou dost judge—as a witness, attest,
        And thou settest thy hand and seal,
    And the winner is blest, and the loser at rest—

(Chorus of all) :

    Hurrah ! for the bright blue steel !

[HUGO *and* ERIC *enter during the last verse of*
the song.

Hugo :

> Boot and saddle, old friend,
> Their defiance they send ;
> Time is short—make an end
>> Of thy song.
> Let the sword in this fight
> Strike as hard for the right
> As it once struck for might
>> Leagued with wrong.
> Ha ! Rollo, thou champest
> Thy bridle and stampest,
> For the rush of the tempest
>> Do'st long ?
> Ho ! the kites will grow fatter
> On the corpses we scatter,
> In the paths where we shatter
>> Their throng :
> Where Osric, the craven,
> Hath reared the black raven
> 'Gainst monks that are shaven
>> And cowl'd ;
> Where the Teuton and Hun sit
> In the track of our onset,
> Will the wolves, ere the sunset,
>> Have howl'd.
> Retribution is good,
> They have revell'd in blood,
> Like the wolves of the wood,
>> They have prowl'd.
> Birds of prey they have been,
> And of carrion unclean,
> And their own nests (I ween)
>> They have foul'd.

Eric :

> Two messengers since
> Yestermorn have gone hence,

And ere long will the Prince
　　　　Bring relief.
Shall we pause ?—they are ten
To our one, but their men
Are ill-arm'd, and scarce ken
　　　　Their own chief;
And for this we give thanks :
Their disorderly ranks,
If assail'd in the flanks,
　　　　Will as lief.
Run as fight—loons and lords.

HUGO :

Mount your steeds ! draw your swords !
Take your places !　My words
　　　　Shall be brief :
Ride round by the valley,
Through pass and gorge sally—
The linden trees rally
　　　　Beneath.
Then, Eric and Thurston,
Their ranks while we burst on,
Try which will be first on
　　　　The heath.

(*Aside*)

Look again, mother mine,
Through the happy starshine,
For my sins do'st thou pine ?
　　　　With my breath,
See ! thy pangs are all done,
For the life of thy son :
Thou shalt never feel one
　　　　For his death.

> [*They all go out but* HUGO, *who lingers to tighten
> his girths.* ORION *appears suddenly in
> the gateway.*

ORION:

> Stay, friend! I keep guard on
> Thy soul's gates: hold hard on
> Thy horse.   Hope of pardon
>> Hath fled!
> Bethink once, I crave thee,
> Can recklessness save thee?
> Hell sooner will have thee
>> Instead.

HUGO:

> Back! My soul, tempest toss'd,
> Hath her Rubicon cross'd:
> She shall fly—saved or lost!
>> Void of dread!
> Sharper pang than the steel,
> Thou, oh, serpent! shalt feel,
> Should I set the bruised heel
>> On thy head.   [*He rides out.*

SCENE—A ROOM IN THE CONVENT TOWER OVERLOOKING THE GATE. URSULA *at the window.* AGATHA *and Nuns crouching or kneeling in a corner.*

URSULA:

> See, Ellinor! Agatha! Anna!
>> While yet for the ladders they wait
> Jarl Osric hath rear'd the black banner
>> Within a few yards of the gate;
> It faces our window, the raven,
>> The badge of the cruel sea-kings,
> That has carried to harbour and haven
>> Destruction and death on its wings.

> Beneath us they throng, the fierce Norsemen,
>> The pikemen of Rudolph behind
> Are mustered, and Dagobert's horsemen
>> With faces to rearward inclined;

G

Come last, on their coursers broad-chestea,
　　Rough-coated, short-pastern'd and strong,
Their casques with white plumes thickly crested,
　　Their lances barb-headed and long:

They come through the shades of the linden,
　　Fleet riders and warhorses hot;
The Normans, our friends—we have sinn'd in
　　Our selfishness, sisters, I wot—
They come to add slaughter to slaughter,
　　Their handful can ne'er stem the tide
Of our foes, and our fate were but shorter
　　Without them.　How fiercely they ride!

And "Hugo of Normandy!"　"Hugo!"
　　"A rescue! a rescue!" rings loud,
And right on the many the few go!
　　A sway and a swerve of the crowd!
A springing and sparkling of sword-blades!
　　A crashing and 'countering of steeds!
And the white feathers fly 'neath their broad blades
　　Like foam flakes! the spear-shafts like reeds!

A NUN (to *Agatha*):
　　Pray, sister!
AGATHA:　　　　Alas! I have striven
　　To pray, but the lips move in vain
When the heart with such terror is riven.
　　Look again, Lady Abbess!　Look again!
URSULA:
　　As leaves fall, by wintry gusts scatter'd,
　　　　As fall by the sickle, ripe ears,
　　As the pines by the whirlwind fall shatter'd,
　　　　As shatter'd by bolt fall the firs,
　　To the right hand they fall! to the left hand
　　　　They yield!　They go down! they give back!

And their ranks are divided and cleft, and
  Dispersed and destroy'd in the track !
Where, stirrup to stirrup, and bridle
  To bridle, down-trampling the slain !
Our friends, wielding swords never idle,
  Hew bloody and desperate lane
Through pikemen so crowded together,
  They scarce for their pikes can find room,
Led by Hugo's gilt crest, the tall feather
  Of Thurston, and Eric's black plume !

A NUN (*to Agatha*):
  Pray, sister !

AGATHA :

     First pray thou, that heaven
Will lift this dull weight from my brain,
  That crushes like crime unforgiven.
Look again, Lady Abbess ! Look again !

URSULA :
  Close under the gates men are fighting
    On foot where the raven is rear'd !
'Neath that sword-stroke, through helm and skull
      smiting,
    Jarl Osric falls, cloven to the beard !
And Hugo the hilt firmly grasping,
  His heel on the throat of his foe,
Wrenches back. I can hear the dull rasping,
  The steel through the bone grating low !
And the raven rocks ! Thurston has landed
  Two strokes well-directed and hard
On the standard pole, wielding two-handed
  A blade crimson'd up to the guard,
Like the mast cut in two by the lightning !
  The black banner topples and falls !
Bewildering ! back-scattering ! affright'ning !
  It clears a wide space next the walls.

A Nun (*to Agatha*) :
> Pray, sister !

Agatha :
>   Does the sinner unshriven,
>   With nought beyond this life to gain,
> Pray for mercy on earth or in heaven ?
>   Look again, Lady Abbess !   Look again !

Ursula :
> The gates are flung open, and straightway,
>   By Ambrose and Cyril led on,
> Our own men rush out through the gateway;
>   One charge, and the entrance is won !
> No ! our foes block the gate and endeavour
>   To force their way in !   Oath and yell,
> Shout and war-cry wax wilder than ever !
>   Those children of Odin fight well ;
> And my ears are confused by the crashing,
>   The jarring, the discord, the din ;
> And mine eyes are perplex'd by the flashing
>   Of fierce lights that ceaselessly spin ;
> So when thunder to thunder is calling,
>   Quick flash follows flash in the shade,
> So leaping and flashing and falling
>   Blade flashes and follows on blade !
> While the sward newly-plough'd, freshly painted,
>   Grows purple with blood of the slain,
> And slippery !   Has Agatha fainted ?

Agatha :
> Not so, Lady Abbess ! Look again !

Ursula :
> No more from the window ; in the old years
>   I have look'd upon strife.   Now I go
> To the court-yard to rally our soldiers
>   As I may—face to face with the foe.
>   [*She goes out.*

SCENE—A Room in the Convent. Thurston *seated near a small fire.*

Enter Eustace.

EUSTACE:

We have come through this skirmish with hardly
a scratch.

THURSTON:

And, without us, I fancy, they have a full batch
Of sick men to look to. Those robbers accurs'd
Will soon put our soundest on terms with our
worst.
Nathless I'd have bartered with never a frown
Ten years for those seconds when Osric went down.
Where's Ethelwolf ?

EUSTACE: Dying.

THURSTON: And Reginald ?

EUSTACE: Dead.

And Ralph is disabled, and Rudolph is sped.
He may last till midnight—not longer. Nor Tyrrel,
Nor Brian, will ever see sunrise.

THURSTON: That Cyril
The monk, is a very respectable fighter.

EUSTACE:

Not bad for a monk. Yet our loss had been lighter,
Had he and his fellows thrown open the gate
A little more quickly. And now, spite of fate,
With thirty picked soldiers, their siege we might
weather,
But the Abbess is worth all the rest put together.
                              [*Enter* URSULA.

THURSTON:

Here she comes.

URSULA: Can I speak with your lord ?

EUSTACE: 'Tis too late,
He was dead when we carried him in at the gate.

THURSTON :

    Nay, he spoke after that, for I heard him myself ; .

    But he won't speak again, he must lie on his shelf.

URSULA :

    Alas ! is he dead, then ?

THURSTON :   As dead as St. Paul.

    And what then ? to-morrow, we too, one and all

    Die, to fatten these ravenous carrion birds.

    I knelt down by Hugo and heard his last words :

    " How heavy the night hangs—how wild the waves

        dash ;

    Say a mass for my soul—and give Rollo a mash."

URSULA :

    . Nay, Thurston, thou jestest.

THURSTON :   Ask Eric. I swear

    We listened, and caught every syllable clear.

EUSTACE :

    Why, his horse was slain too.

THURSTON :   'Neath the linden trees grey,

    Ere the onset, young Henry rode Rollo away ;

    He will hasten the Prince, and they may reach

        your gate

    To-morrow—though to-morrow for us is too late.

    Hugo rode the boy's mare, and she's dead, if you

        like—

    Disembowel'd by the thrust of a freebooter's pike.

EUSTACE :

    Neither Henry nor Rollo we ever shall see.

URSULA :

    But we may hold the walls till to-morrow.

THURSTON :

                         Not we.

    In an hour or less, having rallied their force,

    They'll storm your old building—and take it, of

        course,

Since of us, who alone in war's science are skill'd,
One-third are disabled, and two-thirds are kill'd.

URSULA:

Art thou hurt ?

THURSTON: At present I feel well enough,
But your water is brackish, unwholesome, and
    rough ;
Bring a flask of your wine, dame, for Eustace and I,
Let us gaily give battle, and merrily die.

                    [*Enter* ERIC, *with arm in sling.*

ERIC:

Thou art safe, Lady Abbess ! The convent is safe.
To be robbed of their prey, how the ravens will
    chafe ;
The vanguard of Otto is looming in sight :
At the sheen of their spears, see thy foemen take
    flight.
Their foremost are scarce half a mile from the wall.

THURSTON:

Bring the wine, lest those Germans should swallow
    it all.

SCENE—THE CHAPEL OF THE CONVENT.

(*Dirge of the Monks.*)

Earth to earth, and dust to dust,
    Ashes unto ashes go.
Judge not. He who judgeth just,
    Judgeth merciful also.
Earthly penitence hath fled,
    Earthly sin hath ceased to be ;
Pile the sods on heart and head,
    Miserere Domine !

            Hominum et angelorum,
                Domine ! precamur te
            Ut immemor sis malorum—
                Miserere Domine !
                    (*Miserere !*)

Will the fruits of life brought forth,
  Pride and greed, and wrath and lust,
Profit in the day of wrath,
  When the dust returns to dust?
Evil flower and thorny fruit
  Load the wild and worthless tree,
Lo ! the axe is at the root,
  Miserere Domine !

      Spes, fidesque, caritasque,
        Frustra fatigant per se,
      Frustra virtus, forsque, fasque,
        Miserere Domine !
          (Miserere !)

Fair without and foul within,
  When the honey'd husks are reft
From the bitter sweets of sin,
  Bitterness alone is left,
Yet the wayward soul hath striven
  Mostly hell's ally to be,
In the strife 'twixt hell and heaven,
  Miserere Domine !

      Heu! heu! herbâ latet anguis—
        Caro herba—carni væ—
      Solum purgat, Christi sanguis,·
        Miserere Domine !
          (Miserere !)

Pray that in the doubtful fight
  Man may win through sore distress,
By His goodness infinite,
  And His mercy fathomless.
Pray for one more of the weary
  Head bowed down and bended knee,
Swell the requiem, *Miserere!*
  Miserere Domine !

      Bonum, malum, qui fecisti
        Mali imploramus te,
      Salve fratrem, causâ Christi,
        Miserere Domine !
          (Miserere !)

Clarson, Massina, and Co., Printers, 72 Little Collins Street East, Melbourne.